DATE DUE

OCT. 09 1999	
JUN. 03 2000	
MAR 0 2 2011	

D1517962

WINSTON, DAOMA   THE LONG AND LIVING
SHADOW

DEMCO

The
Long
And
Living
Shadow

Also by Daoma Winston
in Thorndike Large Print ®

The Mayeroni Myth
Castle of Closing Doors
The Carnaby Curse

This Large Print Book carries the
Seal of Approval of N.A.V.H.

The Long And Living Shadow

Daoma Winston

Thorndike Press • Thorndike, Maine

Copyright © 1968 by Daoma Winston.

All rights reserved.

Thorndike Large Print® Romance Series edition published in 1993 by arrangement with Jay Garon Brooke Association, Inc.

The tree indicium is a trademark of Thorndike Press.

Set in 16 pt. News Plantin by Heidi E. Saucier.

This book is printed on acid-free, high opacity paper. ∞

Library of Congress Cataloging-in-Publication Data

Winston, Daoma, 1922-
    The long and living shadow / Daoma Winston.
      p.   cm.
    ISBN 1-56054-729-4 (alk. paper : lg. print)
    1. Large type books.   I. Title.
    [PS3545.I7612L65 1993]
    813'.54—dc20   93-12737
                                                    CIP

For Rita Ann and Frank

1

"There is no antidote to fear but courage, no absolute anodyne for pain but time." Bennett grinned, and his serious face brightened with mischief as he added, "Mayfield's theorem, you know."

Remembering, Mickey Mayfield winced.

Had he been preparing her?

Had he known then what was to come?

Bennett . . . husband and teacher. Herself . . . wife and student.

She knew it would do no good to think such thoughts and sought for diversion.

The cab driver wore a red baseball cap. From below it, thick white curls crept down his neck and around his ears. He controlled the car firmly as it hurtled along the swooping curves of the Capital Beltway.

Mickey peered through the thick mauve haze of late summer twilight. She had forgotten the great fleets of chrome and steel that raced down American roads. There had been few cars on the small lane in the Copenhagen suburb where she had spent the past four years.

Her eyes widened, her bones melted, at the

assault of speed. But the driver was accustomed to it. He was like an insouciant jockey, wearing sunlit silks, astride a powerful stallion. His big dark hands held the wheel lightly, as if it were reins, and lifted the cab to a change of pace, then slowed it to maneuver tight turns.

She sighed. The cab driver was not a jockey in sunlit silks. He was a small, middle-aged Negro man, who whistled softly between his teeth while the meter ticked miles away.

The last time she had seen a horse race was at Epsom Downs, with Bennett. She remembered his solicitous face bent toward her, "You're not too tired, Mickey?" and her, "Oh, Bennett, why should I be?" impatient that the myth of her fragility persisted, determined that it would not, must not.

She should have known then, guessed, sensed, that he was tired.

But in those days, the cocoon of an excessively prolonged childhood still enwrapped her. She was giddy with sunlight, with the unaccustomed sound of English words around her, with the blare of trumpets, the swirl of crowds and color. She wore a yellow dress, and yellow shoes, and all she wanted was for that day to go on and on forever. But it had not, for days never did.

Now she was sitting bolt upright, gripping

8

the back of the driver's seat. Her hands were thin, the wrists fragile. Elegant wrists, Bennett had often said. The diamonds in her engagement ring, her wedding ring, winked at her like malevolent eyes.

She forced herself to lean back, relax. She crossed her slender legs, and fished in her big black patent leather purse for a cigarette. She found one, but forgot to light it, and simply rolled it between her fingers. It was a gesture habitual to her, but she had never recognized it until Bennett pointed it out to her.

The driver offered her matches over the seat, and she took them, thanked him in an almost steady voice. She managed to get the cigarette lit. He told her to keep the matches, so she dropped them in her bag.

As she did, she noticed her skirt, and realized that she was wearing yellow — wearing yellow as she had worn that day at Epsom Downs. She wasn't in mourning because at some time or other — she no longer remembered why the subject had come up — Bennett told her that he didn't believe widows should shroud themselves in black.

She would have preferred it. Mourning clothes would be a shield against the small kindnesses which were actually cruelties to her. She did not want strangers to do for her what Bennett had always done.

But it was completely necessary to her now that she fulfill every one of his desires. As if, somehow or other, she could make up to him for all her earlier failings. The worst of which had been that she never guessed he was ill.

It was like unwarily opening a crowded closet from which brooms and mops leaped out to assail her.

She had not known about Bennett's heart condition. Why? She came in from the garden with her arms full of greenery, and said, "Look how lovely." And then, seeing him nap in the big chair, something he often did, she tiptoed past him to the kitchen. She arranged the bright blossoms, humming to herself. When she heard the whistle of the afternoon postman, and saw the red flash of his coat as he bicycled up the lane, she went to the door. There was no mail.

On the way back to the kitchen, she paused to look at Bennett. He hadn't moved. His head was bent at what seemed a peculiarly uncomfortable angle. She decided to waken him just enough so that he would change position. She whispered, "Bennett, Bennett, dear . . ." She leaned over him, touched his hand. He didn't waken. She knew he would never waken again.

She had an agonizing total recall of the next

few seconds. The drowning sense of loss. The helplessness, the fear. What would she do without Bennett? How would she live?

She managed to call the office. David Neilsen, Bennett's assistant, arrived within a few minutes, and with him, Bennett's doctor.

They seemed to take it as a matter of course that she hadn't known about his heart condition, about the pills she later found in his dresser drawer. They considered her, Bennett's wife of four years, his child bride; delicate, fragile, and always protected.

The rest of that day was blurred. But by the next morning, she knew that she must do exactly as Bennett wanted. He had preferred cremation. Though her flesh shuddered, she made the arrangements, and it was done. He had told her once that some day she would have to go home. Though her flesh shuddered, she began the preparations.

David Neilsen and Bennett's doctor had wanted her to leave immediately. They wanted to pack for her, to close up the house. To do for her all those things that Bennett had always done before. She wouldn't let them help her. Bennett was gone. She would do them herself.

She had managed, perhaps not with the greatest efficiency, but still she had managed to do what had to be done. She discovered that she was not quite as helpless as she had always thought. She discovered that once she got over her fear of making a mistake she could make a decision.

In the month it took her to dispose of the house to which she had come as a bride, she thought about the marriage that death had ended. Even then, she didn't know why she hadn't guessed that Bennett was ill.

The doctor had discovered the condition when Bennett went to him, complaining about chest pains he never mentioned to her. David Neilsen had been told, warned even, it seemed. Only she, protected in the excessively prolonged cocoon of childhood, had been left in the dark. But she should have been alert to the signs, and there were signs, of course. She should have suspected.

Even her aunt, Winifred Warren, that formidable lady never known for sensitivity, had said, "Mickey, are you quite sure that Bennett is all right? He looks overtired to me." And added with what was almost a simper, "But of course, a man that age, and with such a young wife . . ."

"He's only fifty-five," Mickey protested.

"And you're only twenty-three." Winifred sighed. "More than twice your age. Very unsuitable, really. I did try to tell your parents that. But they would give you everything you wanted, whatever it was. It was always like that, wasn't it, Mickey? So when you came home with Bennett . . ."

"Father introduced us himself," Mickey said defensively.

"Oh, yes, that's right, isn't it?" Winifred agreed.

She was a woman of unguessable age, though Mickey assumed she must be a few years older than Bennett. She had great masses of white hair piled into a smooth hive of waves. Her face was like a well-used leather glove, scored by habitual use. Two deep lines cut the pink of her forehead. Two more framed her lightly-painted mouth. Yet she was, in fact, singularly expressionless, and her eyes, the grayish-brown of weathered ice, peered emptily from brackets of well-powdered wrinkles. Her voice was deep and varied in modulation so that some words came out a whisper, and the listener had to lean forward to hear, and other words seemed underscored, which made the listener wonder if some double meaning had passed her by.

"You must," Winifred said, whispering, "be careful of Bennett's health. It is a terrible thing to be left alone."

It had been a bright day, but Winifred managed to dim the sun. A shadow fell over the green and white striped awning of the outdoor

13

café. A hush settled on the crowded Tivoli Gardens.

Mickey wondered if Winifred were referring in an oblique fashion to the death ten months before of Mickey's parents. She wondered why, suddenly, and after so long, Winifred had decided to visit her in Copenhagen.

Mickey, after receiving the cable which announced Winifred's imminent arrival, had cautiously confessed a certain uneasiness to Bennett. "I was always fond of Aunt Winifred and her children, Bennett. I really was. But it's been so long. And . . . oh, Bennett, suppose she keeps remembering what happened? Suppose she looks at me as if . . ."

Bennett had said then, "You're still not quite sure, are you?"

"I am," she cried. "I am all right. I'm fine. I know it."

But he said thoughtfully, "Some day you're going to have to go back, go home, Mickey. The only way to resolve doubt is to search for certainty."

"Some day," she agreed, though she shuddered inside, and hoped that Bennett didn't notice. "Yes. Some day."

"As for Winifred . . . we'll see that she has a pleasant stay. She and her children, after all, are the only family you have, Mickey."

Her only family . . . and even them, not

14

really. Winifred was some kind of cousin, a Bassett before she married a Warren, and related by blood, though distantly, to Mickey's father.

Widowed when young, with three small children, Winifred and her family had lived with the Bassetts in the big house called Bassett Place. Then, when Mickey was fourteen, there had been the small unpleasantness, as Mickey's mother later called it, and the Warrens moved away. Mickey preferred to leave all memory of that time safely forgotten. Besides, the breach had healed over the years, and the Warrens had been very kind to her and helpful to Bennett, when they had gone back when her parents died.

Winifred arrived, and Mickey was delighted to find that the old fondness remained. If Winifred remembered the small unpleasantness in the year that Mickey was fourteen, it didn't show. Winifred settled down to enjoy her vacation.

In spite of her age, she was a big, robust woman with inexhaustible fountains of energy. She led Mickey through endless miles of sightseeing on the Stroet, to Nyhavn, to the fish markets, and copper markets, and wood markets. And, always, back to the Tivoli, where that day, having expressed concern for Bennett's health, she surveyed the

15

exotic skyline, the pagodas, and domes, and dismissed them. "A child's dream of fairyland. You'd think these people would grow up." Then she poked a fork into the open sandwich she had ordered, "For the life of me I can't see why they don't eat real sandwiches."

"This is their way."

Winifred shrugged. Her grayish-brown eyes sharpened on something behind Mickey. "Quick, look, those adorable twins."

Mickey turned, staring into the crowd that ambled along the flower-lined paths. She saw no twins. She turned back to Winifred.

Winifred gave her a self-satisfied smile. "You missed them? No matter, dear. There are plenty of twins in the world."

Mickey remembered that Winifred had always been preoccupied with twins. Duplicate dolls decorated her dressing table in the old house when Mickey was a child. There had been a time when Winifred dressed her sons, Alexander and Noah, alike. And another when she had bought identical dresses, one for her daughter Theodora, and one for Mickey. But Mickey's mother, usually so gentle and giving, had been remarkably firm. The dress for Mickey was put away, never seen again, although Mickey, impressed by the pink ruffles, had cried. But Winifred's preoccupation with twins had not faded. And perhaps, Mickey

16

thought, with age, as sometimes happens, Winifred might be growing a bit odd.

But, odd or not, she had guessed that Bennett was ill, while Mickey had gone on living in her child's paradise for two more months . . .

Now, in the cab, she found herself once again sitting bolt upright, gripping the seat before her.

"Traffic bother you, miss? Don't worry. I can run along here with my eyes shut and know where I'm going and get there, too."

"I'm not used to it."

"You just coming for a visit?"

"No. I'm home for good now."

The words gave her a queer little shiver of terror. She had never really expected to return. She had imagined that her life with Bennett would go on and on. As she had wanted that day at Epsom to go on and on.

"Lots of changes," he said. "Two years since the Beltway's been running . . . Yep, lots of changes."

She agreed, thinking that without Bennett's strong arm to lean on, everything would indeed be different.

Just a year before, at her parents' death, she and Bennett had come back together. He rented a car. They went straight to the Willard Hotel.

"This isn't a hick town any more," the driver said. "I was born and bred in Washington. So I know."

"So was I," she told him.

On that last trip, she and Bennett had very little time. The funeral, a visit with Winifred and her children . . . Mickey remembered weeping while Bennett took care of that great mass of detail which had to be handled. She wished now that she had listened. Though Bennett was gone, the mass of detail remained.

"Two natives in the same car!" the driver said. "That doesn't happen often. This is a transients' town. But me, I was raised down next to the river. You can't see the place any more. But a shantytown was there in those days, and wasn't gone until just after the war." He gave her a look in the rear view mirror and chuckled. "I mean the Second World War. You wouldn't know about that. You're too young. You wouldn't even remember those little shacks. But people lived in them. People with chickens and dogs, and a million kids it seemed like." He sighed. "Yep, changes. It's all gone now."

"That must have been near where I grew up," she said. "We lived on the Palisades, in Bassett Place."

"Bassett Place? That's where I worked when I was a kid. Is that where you want

18

to go? You only said MacArthur Boulevard just inside the District Line."

"I didn't think you'd know it."

"Sure. I know it. I mowed many a lawn there, and scrubbed the screens." He frowned into the rear view mirror. "But it's all closed up now, has been for a year. Ever since old Mr. Benjamin Bassett died, and his wife with him, and . . ." The driver's voice trailed off. "You don't want to go there, miss."

She smoothed the yellow skirt over her knees. She swallowed hard. She suddenly knew that he was right. She didn't want to go home. She didn't want to resolve doubt by searching for certainty. And anyway, she told herself insistently, there was no doubt to resolve. But her life with Bennett was over. And he had wanted her, one day, to go home.

"You must be the little girl," the driver was saying. "You came later, after I went to school, and away to war." He chuckled, "Talk about coincidences . . ."

The words plucked some tightly drawn string in her. She shuddered. She did not believe in coincidences. Yet Bennett had always said one must allow for the vagaries of fate. She reminded herself of that, and yet, she asked herself how it could be that a taxi cab driver, chosen at random in the airport by the daughter of Benjamin Bassett, could turn out to be a man who had once worked for Benjamin Bassett. She could find no answer. Coincidence then.

"Your folks were good people," the driver was saying. "And you're their little girl, all grown up now, and coming home."

"Yes. I'm all grown up," she said, smiling.

"Only the place is closed, like I told you. You don't want to go there yet. I'll take you to a nice hotel. You can settle down there, until you make whatever arrangements you need to."

She wondered briefly what there was about her that made everyone, even strangers, feel that they must take care of her. She knew she must learn to take care of herself. That was why she had notified only the real estate people that she was coming back. That was why she had not even answered Alexander's importunate letter, nor Winifred's cable, though it was good of both of them to have been concerned.

She said, with more confidence than she felt, "The house will be open. Electricity and phone turned on. And I have the key."

The house key, neatly labeled in Bennett's precise handwriting, had been in the top drawer of his desk, waiting for her to need it. Now it was in her purse, secured by a rubber band to the small bottle of pills that had belonged to Bennett. Mickey did not know why she had carefully kept the pills. They were a final symbol of her marriage. She had been, quite simply, unable to throw them out.

"If you have the key," the driver said, "it'll be all right."

She hoped it would be. She fished nervously in her purse for another cigarette, and got it lit with the driver's matches.

"You'll be there soon."

The queer little shiver of terror went through her.

She reached for a cigarette, realized that she was already smoking one, and put the lit one out, and the unused one away.

She looked through the deepening twilight. The Potomac River flowed wide and still. Next to it, but separated by an uneven swath of green, the canal was a flat, narrow ribbon.

The canal . . . She and her father. She could see herself running ahead, turning back to shout to him. He following, leaned on his cane, and smiled into the sunlight. He had been very tall, white-haired, and looked like the judge he had once been.

"We walked there, my father and I, a long time ago."

"Not all that long ago. You're not much more than a little girl still."

She gave her head an impatient shake. She

had been orphaned, been widowed. She had wept until she felt each tear to be a drop of life's blood. She had known depths of fear she thought to be the bottom of hell. Yet none of it had left a mark on her. The scars were within, within.

She sighed, looked out the window as the cab swung in a careful turn into a suddenly familiar street, and sped up a hill and turned again, and then again as the street lights suddenly bloomed against the heavy blue of the twilight.

"See? I know my way all right to Bassett Place."

The cab drifted by the tall iron fence, rolled on to the ornate gate at the center of the block. There, under the flickering flame of two gas lamps, it came to a gentle stop.

Mickey sat forward, trembling.

She was home.

2

The small blue gas flames danced over the gateposts.

Watching them, Mickey was filled with sweet swift joy.

It was Runyon, small, dwarfed Runyon of the pinkish hair and pinkish skin, who had told her long before, "The lamps never go out, Mickey. Day and night they shine, saying all is well at Bassett Place."

"But they can be turned off, can't they?" she demanded, more to keep him talking than to know.

"Sure. They can be. There's a pipe to each one, and a little gismo on it. Twist that, and away go the lamps of Bassett Place."

Runyon, along with his sister Bevis, had worked for the Warren family for years, and with them, he had come to live on the Palisades. When they left, Runyon left, too.

It had been a long time since Mickey had thought of him. There was sweet swift joy in remembering him. But that joy was gone when she looked past the flickering lamps to the house.

It was dark, still, shadowed by the giant

oak trees that spread ancient limbs around it.

There were two stories, but the attic had been converted by dormers into a third floor. One huge bright room full of ells and angles had been Mickey's special province and sanctuary.

The first floor was surrounded by wide porches that wore wisteria and honeysuckle vines, rich and thick and fragrant like scented scarves.

Mickey couldn't see it, but at the back would be the old stable that had been converted into a two-car garage, and above it, the apartment for servants where Runyon and Bevis once lived.

"Gate's closed," the driver said, pushing back his red baseball cap. "Don't see any lights."

Mickey thought helplessly that she had no key large enough to fit the huge lock of the closed gates. She asked herself what to do.

"We'll see," the driver said. He got out. A moment later, he grinned at her, and swung the gate open. He returned, drove through. "Only why it should be so dark . . ."

"Nobody knew what time I would be arriving," she told him, as he maneuvered up the circular driveway.

But when he stopped before the steps, he said, "I don't see why you'd want to go in there now. I'll take you to a hotel, and —"

She fumbled in her purse, came up with the key. "It's all right."

He got out and went around to open the door for her. He gave her a surprised look when she stood beside him. "You're so little. Hardly five three, aren't you? And my daughter, Mallie, she's twelve, and your size already."

Mickey smiled, but her face felt tight, her lips dry. "Maybe that's when I stopped growing."

She had a tiny yellow straw hat perched on her short black curls. Her yellow silk suit fit her as if she had always been slender, but she had recently become downright thin. Her face was all eyes and obvious cheek bones and pointed chin. She felt, then, very much like a frightened child, trying to convince herself that she was grown up by dressing in her mother's clothes.

He got her two bags from the trunk, and Mickey followed him when he carried them up to the porch.

He looked past her at the two dark windows that flanked the door. Suddenly, he frowned. "I'll take your bags inside for you."

"That's not necessary." She brought out a five dollar bill.

"It's no bother. Not for Mr. Benjamin

Bassett's girl." He looked at the windows, frowning again.

She saw what she thought might be a flicker of light inside. But she said insistently, "It's all right."

She wanted to be alone. That was the thing. She didn't know why. But she had to go in alone.

The driver gave her a hurt look. He pulled a card from his pocket. "You keep this. If you want a cab, you call the company, and ask for me. Ben Johnson. I'll be glad to drive you. Anywhere, any time. O.K.?"

She accepted the card and thanked him. She waited until he had gotten into the cab before she turned to the door. She unlocked it and pushed. It seemed to stick. When she pressed harder, it slammed inward.

She leaped back and stumbled and caught herself. Then she stood still, paralyzed by a familiar fear. Around her, the hot breathing silence was a cloud of heavy air scented with honeysuckle and wistaria.

She had wanted to go in alone. It was a point of honor with her, she had thought. Now she knew that she simply hadn't trusted herself, hadn't known how she would behave. She wanted no witnesses . . . in case . . . which was why she had refused the Warrens' repeated offers of help, and the cab driver's too.

Yet now she wished she had someone with her. Someone who could find the switch for the chandelier so that light would scatter the twilight shadows from the big hall.

She had believed — she had wanted to believe — that the old familiar fear was gone.

Now, sighing, she admitted the truth to herself.

That vague sense of hovering disaster, like the fluttering of huge black bat wings just beyond her vision, had persisted. It was, she knew, a residue of the breakdown she had had in her teens. All that was left of those months of weeping, of imagined whisperings, of thinking she saw the flicker of watching eyes. The sense of hovering disaster, the feeling that she was an alien intruder in her own home.

She knew that she was well, had been for years, what was once weakness converted to strength. But Bennett had known her doubt when she had not known it herself.

Here, in Bassett Place, she had walked in the valley of long and living shadows, and screamed in madness, and finally wept and fought her way once again into sunlight.

And it was here that she must search for the certainty to resolve her doubt. She must prove to herself that she would never stumble

27

back into the valley of long and living shadows.

For this was home.

It belonged to her. And she belonged to it.

The house was utterly still.

She couldn't remember having heard such a stillness before.

Her own breath was an intrusion.

She was herself an intruder.

There was a sudden whisper in the oak trees and the wistaria vines.

She turned quickly to look behind her. Nothing moved, no one was about. Only the breeze moved, bringing night mist from the river below. The gaslights glimmered faintly at the gate. As she watched, the cab passed under a distant street lamp, turned and disappeared.

In winter, she remembered, when the trees were bare, the river was visible from the porch. She thought of the fine sunsets she had watched, and remembered that she had seen them, not from the porch, but from the dormer windows of her top floor room during the long months of her illness.

She turned back to the door, trying to recall the location of the chandelier switch. She could see it in her mind, an ornate plate, carved copper edges and fluting. But where?

She told herself that it was quite natural to

have forgotten. She had actually been in the house only rarely since she had gone away to school. She had traveled with her parents during vacation. They had always known of the memories the house aroused in her, and encouraged her to stay away.

Just a few months after she was graduated, her father, having met Bennett through mutual friends, introduced him to Mickey. They had been delighted that the chance meeting had produced love, and happy when Mickey married Bennett and went with him to Copenhagen, where he headed a large export-import firm.

In the four years of her marriage, she had seen them only once. With the wisdom of hindsight, she knew that they had come to visit her as soon as they learned her father was incurably ill. They had not told her. Her last memories of them were sweet. She thought, then, that because they were both elderly they were relieved to see her safely settled in life. Now she understood more. Returning home, her mother had nursed her husband until the end, and apparently, once his eyes were closed for good, she took him into her arms and swallowed the pills that would allow her to follow him into death.

Mickey took a deep gulp of air and reached inside, feeling along the wall. Her fingers found the switch, pulled it.

Instantly the big hall bloomed with light from the huge crystal chandelier. The shadows fled away.

She smiled and got her bags and brought them in. She closed the door behind her, and as she turned, she caught a flash of movement from the corner of her eye.

She gasped, and swung around. She stared at the small girl who stared back at her.

For a moment, huge black bat wings seemed to hover near her. The familiar fear engulfed her.

She fought it. She told herself that there was nothing to be afraid of.

But suddenly she imagined that she heard her father's voice, deep, angry, "But what a terribly cruel thing to do to a child." And her mother weeping. And Winifred, choked on sobs. "But I didn't mean . . . I didn't think . . . it just happened to pop out . . ."

Tears burned Mickey's eyes. Why think of that? A moment out of the past. It had nothing to do with now. What she felt was simply an echo of a fear once known, but overcome.

Still, she shuddered. The small girl shuddered.

She made herself laugh. The small girl laughed. "Mickey," she cried aloud. "Oh, you dope, Mickey Bassett Mayfield!"

The small girl silently cried words back at her from the wide, gold-framed mirror.

"All right," Mickey said. "I'll teach you to scare the life out of me. Now go away." She turned her back, smiling easily by then.

Suddenly, for no reason at all, the crystal chandelier set up a soft whispering sound.

She stared at the faint shadows that moved along the wall, and held her breath, but she saw nothing. There was nothing to see.

She put her purse on the table under the mirror. She took off her small yellow straw hat and placed it carefully next to her purse.

Her pale face, all eyes and cheek bones and pointed chin, stared back at her.

She smiled. "You're home, Mickey. This is the beginning. You're home now."

She wasn't sure what she meant by those words, but they comforted her.

She looked at her two suitcases, decided that they could be unpacked later. And much later, of course, the rest of her things would be arriving by sea freight.

If there were lights, she reasoned, there would be gas in the kitchen as well. She would make herself a cup of tea, and sit down, and have a cigarette, and consider what to do next.

But first she would turn on more lights. She went to the double doors of the living room.

They were closed. She couldn't remember ever having seen them closed before. She tugged at the brass handles and the doors slid soundlessly on their tracks, opening to admit her.

But she stood perfectly still.

The huge room was dark, empty except for the faint outlines of sheet-covered furniture hulking in the shadows.

But something, someone was there.

She took a step back, hands still on the doors, her throat so dry that she could not swallow.

She noticed a scent, not the wistaria and honeysuckle from outside, but a sweet rich perfume that reminded her of a woman dressed in furs, and which overpowered the mustiness of a house old and unoccupied for a long time.

She groped for the light, and found it, and as the chandelier came alive, she saw the faint trails of smoke rising and fading away.

She watched until the wisps dissolved, and finally then, she whispered hoarsely, like a child awakening from a nightmare. "Who's there? Who's there?"

A faint sigh answered her, a creak of springs.

More loudly, she cried, "Who's there?"

A dark spot appeared against the white sheet that hung over the sofa before the fire place.

The sheet twisted and pulled. The dark spot rose higher, became the back of a well-shaped head. It turned and became a face, and burning black eyes stared at her.

She waited blindly, unable to move.

The black eyes were bottomless. She saw into them and saw nothing. She thought, I'm afraid. I'm terribly afraid. This is the valley of long and living shadow.

The room seemed to jerk and spin, to sail around like a child's top, then slowly to settle at rest, while distant discordant music faded.

Her hazy vision cleared.

She knew the man before her.

He was standing by then, the sofa between them.

She was ridiculously glad of that barrier. If it had not been there, she might have shamed herself by collapsing into his arms.

He said in a deep, mocking voice, "Mickey, surely you haven't forgotten me so soon."

3

Her breath, frozen until then, melted in her throat. She gasped, "Noah! Noah Warren!"

The faint mockery faded swiftly from his black eyes. He came toward her, hands outstretched, full of an intent anxiety. "Mickey, are you all right?"

"Yes. Oh, yes. Of course, I am. But I thought . . ."

"You thought what?"

He was watching her too closely.

She began again. "It was such a surprise to see you, Noah."

"I'm sorry. I didn't mean to frighten you. I was waiting for you, and thinking. I guess the thinking bored me. I fell asleep."

"It's just that . . . somehow, coming home . . . this house . . ." She stopped herself, gave him an uncertain look, then turned away, hoping to hide her sudden embarrassment.

She wondered if he, too, were thinking of that moment in the garden of her Copenhagen house, when suddenly, for no reason that she knew, there had seemed to be something strange and compelling between them, and she had realized how easy it was for her to talk

to him, to blurt out what she could never say to anyone else.

If he were remembering that moment, there was no sign of it on his face. There was a skeptical twist in his mouth. The mockery was back in his eyes. He said, "Why should I evoke such terror in you, Mickey?"

"You? Oh, no."

"Or make you want to run away?"

"But I'm not running away."

He grinned. "You're hovering at the threshold. Why don't you come in. Make yourself at home. After all, I have."

But she stayed where she was near the door, waiting for the return of calmness which seemed too long in coming.

He looked down at his still outstretched hands, then jammed them in his pockets. His grin was gone. He seemed, suddenly, aglow with white-lipped fury.

He was wearing chinos, a gray shirt, sandals. His short dark hair was tousled.

Noah, Bennett had said, affected a faintly disreputable air as an antidote to Winifred's pride and Alexander's pomposity, and Theodora's petulance. One day, Bennett chuckled, Noah would outgrow that need and find himself to be a man. But now, Mickey thought, he was twenty-seven years old. If he were to outgrow that need, then it was time and time overdue.

He said, "Alexander called me. The real estate people had let him know you were coming in. He had another appointment and couldn't get here. So I had to get the key, and be a welcoming committee of one. I'm sorry if the welcoming committee isn't welcome."

"I wondered how you knew I'd be arriving."

"Now you don't have to wonder." He went on, "And following Alexander's explicit directions, I brought you a box full of groceries, now in the kitchen, and the flowers, and . . ."

The flowers. Tall carnations, pink, white, and red . . . the rich scent — Winifred's favorite. And Noah's cigarette, smoldering in the ashtray, while he dozed on the sheet-covered sofa.

A draft touching the chandelier, a rich scent, a drift of smoke . . . Those were the things of which her fear was made when she thrust open the doors of the room.

Smiling now, she murmured, "Alexander thought of everything."

"My wonderful brother. Yes," Noah agreed. "He always does."

"It was kind of him. And of you, Noah."

"You don't think so at all, Mickey." Noah grinned. "You wanted to slip in, alone and unremarked. There was quite a to-do in the family about it."

"Not really, Noah," she protested, feeling guilt.

"Yes, really. I was all for giving you your own way. Theodora . . ." Noah shrugged. "You know Theodora. But my mother, and Alexander . . . when they make up their minds. Not to mention Runyon. Between them, and Alexander's call . . . here I am, and at your service, too. What can I do for you?"

"Why . . . why, nothing. I'll just get settled down."

"And what?"

"I haven't had a chance to think ahead, Noah."

He said soberly, "I'm sorry about Bennett. I never thought when we visited you in June that such a thing could happen."

She nodded, unable to answer him.

"It was very sudden, wasn't it?"

She nodded again.

"I didn't think you'd come here, though."

"Why not?"

He paused, studying her, still sober. "You've spent little time here, haven't you?"

"The way it worked out," she said hastily.

"Since you were sick. It's got to do with that."

She protested, "No, it hasn't. And besides, that's all over with."

"It is?"

"Of course, Noah. What do you mean?"

"I wondered . . . when I saw your face as you came in . . ."

She gave a shaky laugh. "Oh, that. But you see, I never dreamed anyone would be here. And there was no car outside. So . . ."

"I parked out back. The key was for the back door."

"Well, it was a surprise to find someone here."

He didn't look convinced, but he didn't say any more about that. Instead, he said, "I think I'd better give you some warning."

She felt a quick hot tingle of alarm. "Warning, Noah?"

But he grinned. "Since you wouldn't let any of us come to help you in Copenhagen, and you didn't notify us directly that you were coming home, I conclude that you intend to keep your distance from the Warrens, Mickey." His grin was warm, approving. "And that's why I'd better warn you. Mother, Winifred, can be pretty overpowering. I'm sure you remember that. So . . ." He shrugged. "I'm afraid you're going to have to be firm."

She grinned back at him. "And I'm afraid you have the wrong idea completely, Noah.

I wasn't trying to keep my distance from the Warrens. You, the rest of them, are all the family I have. I just felt that I should handle everything myself."

"Very commendable," he said dryly, the warm approval suddenly gone. "And I just felt I ought to tell you that Winifred will try to mother you right out of your skin . . . as she's done with the rest of us." He went on, "Never say I didn't mention it. And . . . now, suppose I fix us something to drink. What would you like? Tea. That's what you always drank in Copenhagen, I remember. Or a long, cold, strong one to celebrate your return?"

"A long, cold, strong one, if it's available, thank you."

He jerked a sheet off the sofa, folded it neatly. "There's a place for you to relax while I attend to the refreshments."

She waited until he had started out the side door before she went to sit down. She didn't know why, but she had felt it necessary to keep a certain distance between them.

She found a cigarette and lit it, and suddenly remembered his outstretched hands greeting her, the look on his face, and the terribly strong sensation she had had that she must not touch him.

But when he came back, he handed her a drink and his fingers brushed hers.

That moment in Copenhagen was real again, her strange terror in the hall distant and far away. She was caught in a sense of compelling closeness; said, "Noah, I'm awfully glad to see you. And I don't . . . I hope the family isn't offended by the way I've acted. But when Bennett died, I realized that I've always been so sheltered, so taken care of. I have to learn . . . I want to be . . ." Her voice trailed off.

"Free?" he asked, supplying the word she hadn't said. "On your own. Grown up?"

She nodded. "All that. Yes."

"You needn't look so frightened about it," he grinned. His face relaxed again into warm approval. "It's the most natural feeling in the world, Mickey. There comes a time when a person, I mean a real person, not a dummy, wants to know he's his own man, or, in your case, her own woman."

She knew that he was talking about himself as well as about her. For the first time, she understood that he wasn't trying to be disreputable only to annoy Winifred. He was simply living the way he wanted to.

"Do you know what you want to do yet?" he was asking.

"No." She looked around the big room. "First the house, I think. I must decide about the house."

"Sell it, Mickey."

She shook her head. "I don't know. But I don't think I want to do that."

"Why keep a big old white elephant like this?"

"It's always been in the family, Noah."

"That's not a good reason."

"I like the house."

He said slowly, "Mickey, you loathe it."

"No," she protested.

"No?" He shrugged, lifted his glass. "To a happy homecoming then."

She smiled at him. "Thank you, Noah."

"I'm going to finish this fast, and get out while I can." He smiled back. "Winifred and Alexander will probably be here soon. If you want to duck out on them, I'll take you wherever you want to go."

"Oh, no. I want to see them, Noah."

"Then it's on your head, Mickey."

"What's on my head?"

"The long hours to come. You have my sympathy." He paused to listen. "Yes. See, I was right. There's the car now. I'm going to slip out the back way. You don't mind, do you? I should think one less Warren to handle would be a relief to you." He set down his glass. "If there's anything I can do, call me. I'm in the book. Good luck."

Before she could protest, before she could even thank him, he had gently touched her cheek, and hurried out.

The room was unaccountably empty, silent, with him gone.

She got to her feet, put her barely touched drink aside.

The chandelier whispered faintly as she walked across the room and into the hall.

The car stopped at the steps, the motor died.

She drew a deep breath, and opened the door.

"Oh, there you are, my poor dear," Winifred cried. She came, like a ship under full sail, surging up to the porch.

Alexander and Theodora trailed her, dingies on short lines.

Winifred seized Mickey. "Oh, how sad. How terrible for you. Little did I dream when I saw Bennett, though I did say he looked tired, you do remember that, don't you? I did say he looked tired. But little did I dream what was to happen so soon afterward."

Mickey winced, suffered herself to be hugged, caressed, crooned over.

Finally, Winifred let her go, saying, "And here are your cousins, Mickey."

Alexander, medium height, thick in the shoulder and waist, blond and round-faced, hugged her firmly. "I'm glad to see you again, Mickey. I just wish the circumstances were happier."

Theodora mumbled something and kissed the air near Mickey's cheek. Theodora was blond, too, and plump, and her heavily made-up face was as peculiarly expressionless as Winifred's. She was twenty-five, Winifred's youngest child and as pampered, protected, Mickey suddenly realized, as Mickey herself had always been.

Winifred was saying, "Shall we go in then?" She went ahead, as if she, rather than Mickey, were the hostess. "This lovely place. But so rundown. Now, where is Noah? Don't tell me that he didn't . . ."

"He was here," Mickey said hastily. "Waiting for me when I arrived. It was very kind of you to —"

"And with the — ?"

"The box of groceries, yes, and the carnations. Thank you, Alexander," Mickey added, with a smile at him.

"But where then is Noah?" Winifred demanded.

"He left a few minutes ago."

Winifred sighed. "I don't know what I'm going to do with that boy."

"Give up," Theodora suggested.

She was wearing pale gray linen, a two-piece ensemble. The skirt pulled at her round hips, and she kept smoothing it fretfully.

Winifred, still ahead, swung from the hall

into the living room, saying, "You can't imagine, Mickey, what a trial children can be."

Alexander cut in, "I hope you'll forgive me for having sent Noah here, Mickey, instead of coming myself. It was a business appointment. Nothing else could possibly have kept me away. You do understand?"

She was somewhat taken aback by his earnestness. She smiled, said that she did understand, and at the same time, she thought that she was beginning now to see that Noah was considered an outsider by his family.

Winifred paused in the living room. She gave the big crystal chandelier an admiring glance, then turned, surveying the long room. "Yes, lovely. Though I must say, Mickey, I don't see why you had to come here. This place is a mess. You ought to have written, let us know. You could have easily come to us. And why you didn't give us warning. Tell us your plans . . ."

"I haven't made any plans, not yet."

"But, my dear child, you must have some idea of what you want to do."

"I need a little time to find my feet, I'm afraid."

"Noah didn't uncover the furniture, nor open the windows, nor . . ." Winifred's voice trailed away. Her expressionless face somehow conveyed a frown. "He did manage to serve drinks I see."

"I suggested it," Mickey told her.

Theodora sank into the sofa. "We could do with some drinks."

Her mother ignored her. "At least you haven't unpacked, Mickey. We can go back to our apartment now in that case."

"But I'm going to stay here," Mickey said.

Not that Winifred's suggestion didn't appeal to her. It appealed to her too much. But she felt that she must stay in the house. She must get used to it as quickly as possible.

"Here?" Winifred cried. "But you need someone with you. Servants to clear out this place. And there's Runyon and Bevis, so anxious to see you, dear."

"Perhaps tomorrow . . ."

Winifred went on, "Of course, our apartment is not really large, nor the most delightful, and it will be a bit crowded for you. But under the circumstances it will be better than here. At least you will be with us, instead of alone."

Alexander, perched on an arm of the sofa, murmured, "Mother, please . . . if Mickey feels . . ."

But Winifred was staring at the mantel. She said softly, "Why, my little twin dogs are still there, after all this time. Don't you remember, children? Still there from when we lived here in Bassett Place. And here we are, together again, just as we were then."

Alexander asked, "Mickey, isn't there anything we can do to help you?"

"Not just yet, Alexander. But thank you."

Winifred demanded, "You're not seriously thinking of staying here permanently, are you, Mickey? You can't be!"

"Why not, Aunt Winifred?"

"But, my dear. Alone? It doesn't make sense. Surely you're not strong enough to run this whole house. And then . . . then . . . ?"

Mickey avoided looking directly into Winifred's gray-brown eyes, lest she see there the question she was already asking herself.

Could she live in Bassett Place?

Did she dare?

Or would the long and living shadow reach from the past into the present to destroy her?

A chill went over her.

She swallowed, said quietly, "I want to think about it."

Winifred drew on black lace gloves, a quick, practical gesture. "We'll do what we can to help, of course. You'll need servants . . . I'll see to that for you."

Alexander laughed indulgently. "You're taking Mickey's breath away, Mother."

"Of course," Winifred went on, ignoring his remarks, "if you insist on staying here,

Mickey, then we shall move in with you. That's understood. You need someone to look after you. And we are your only relatives."

Mickey, startled, taken aback, yet at the same time, touched that Winifred should be so interested in her welfare, thought that Bennett would, no doubt, have approved of such an arrangement. But she said, "First we'll have to see about the house."

"If there's nothing for us to do here now, then we shall go. Alexander, Theodora?" Winifred surged toward the hall, her children trailing her. She paused, and they paused. "Mickey, have a good rest. I'll see you first thing tomorrow for a long talk."

"Fine."

"And you're sure, dear? Sure that you do want to stay here alone? You mustn't try to . . . try to pretend, you know. If you're uneasy . . . if . . ."

"I'll be all right," Mickey said. "Really, Aunt Winifred, I'm quite grown up now."

"You are, dear, aren't you?" She went on. In the hall, she paused again. "This dear house . . . so many memories . . ." Suddenly, stopping, she swung back to look at Mickey. "That old unpleasantness so many years ago . . . you realize, of course, that it was all forgotten? On my side, and on your parents' side as well. They understood, my dear. Truly, they did."

"Of course, I know that, Aunt Winifred."

"A foolish word," Winifred sighed. "Spoken in a thoughtless moment."

"It's all in the past now, Aunt Winifred."

"Oh, I'm so glad, my dear. We're all you have left in this world. You are all we have left. We must be close, close and loving always, Mickey." Winifred gave Mickey a quick cheek kiss, a smile, and went to the door.

Alexander hugged Mickey to him, smiled at her, his blue eyes shining into hers. He whispered, in a voice colored with more than cousinly warmth, "I'm so glad you're here."

Theodora grinned. "That's a pretty suit you're wearing, Mickey."

She was relieved when the three of them had gone. She stayed in the open doorway, watching until they had driven through the gate.

She smiled at the flickering gaslights before she went indoors.

The house seemed to settle and sigh around her.

Her pulse quickened. Familiar fear prickled along her skin.

It was all in the past, she had just told Winifred.

But now, alone, she knew that the past threw a long and living shadow, a shadow that did not fade.

4

She shrugged away that thought, and the prickle of fear.

She locked the front door, then went into the living room. The covered furniture looked cold, unfriendly. She stripped the sheets, folded them neatly and stacked them on the sofa. Leaving a trail of lights behind her through drawing room, dining room, and kitchen, she locked the back door, remembering how Noah had hastened away to avoid seeing his family.

On the return trip, she darkened each room as she went, pausing only to look at the twin glass dogs on the mantel in the living room. Winifred's mementos. There would probably be others scattered through the house.

When she turned off the chandelier, the room was full of shadows. She turned her back on them. She took up her two bags, looked along the wide stairway. It seemed to stretch endlessly upward, to disappear into the darkness of the second floor.

A sense of weakness almost overwhelmed her, but she refused to give in to it.

She told herself that she was tired after the

long trip tense with the strain of coming home, of remembering.

She went up the stairs slowly, carefully putting one foot above the other, her eyes on the bright black points of her patent leather shoes.

She was gasping for breath by the time she reached the top. She paused in the faint light from below. She found the chandelier switch, and pink light spilled reassuringly around her. As she started up the more narrow second flight to her old room, she looked at a door near the end of the corridor.

She took a step towards it, then stopped herself.

She remembered the moment. The room, the words, the sharp assault of hurt, followed by numbing shock.

She had been fourteen then, the cherished only child of middle-aged parents. A dreamy, vulnerable, sensitive fourteen . . .

She was in that room at the end of the corridor full of pink light. She with Winifred. Alexander and Noah were both away at the Ivy League college to which Mickey's father had sent them. Theodora was at finishing school. Mickey's parents were visiting old friends in Georgetown.

Winifred and Mickey sat in that picture-cluttered, miniature-cluttered room, and there, talking about the family, Winifred had sighed, "The Bassetts have always been important. Important and respected. As well as wealthy. Such a shame to see the family die out."

"But it isn't dying out, Aunt Winifred," Mickey said artlessly. "There's me."

"But that's not the same," Winifred told her. "How can it be?"

"But it is the same. How can it not be?"

Winifred didn't hear the question. She murmured, "A proud name, a great fortune. I'm the only one left. I, and my children. It's blood lines that count, Mickey. Not papers. Papers don't really change anything. Bassetts are made by blood, by inheritance, by genes. Not by adoption papers."

"Adoption papers?" Mickey whispered, through lips suddenly numb.

Winifred said, "What?" as if she had just remembered that Mickey was sitting there, listening to her. "What?"

"But who is adopted?" Mickey asked. "What did you mean?"

"What did I mean?" Winifred hedged, moving her smooth hands nervously, the horizontal wrinkles on her forehead deepening, the bracketing wrinkles around her mouth etched in acid.

Mickey waited, hardly able to breathe.

Winifred said at last, "Why, nothing. Nothing at all, dear child. I was just thinking aloud, I suppose. It doesn't concern you."

"But it does concern me, doesn't it?" Mickey whispered, unwilling to pursue the subject, yet unable to let it go. "Am I adopted, Aunt Winifred? Aren't . . . aren't Mother and Father . . . my parents? Aren't . . . the Bassetts my parents?"

Winifred equivocated, a look of sheer fright in her eyes. "My dear child . . ."

It was enough.

Mickey rose to walk upon a floor that shook beneath her tentative footsteps. She fumbled her way out of the room, not hearing Winifred's hasty and unconvincing denials.

She crept up the narrow steps to her room, hearing the faint beginning of whispers, feeling the first stares of watching eyes.

The house which had always been her home was telling her the same truth that Winifred had told her.

She was not a Bassett.

She did not belong there.

She was an intruder, and would always be.

Then who was she?

From where had she come?

Who were her rightful parents?

Why hadn't they loved her, wanted her?

The questions began in numbed shock and

grew and multiplied.

Her parents found her later that day. She huddled in the big chair before the dormer window. Her eyes, dry, burning, were fixed in an unseeing stare on the river below.

As soon as her mother touched her, Mickey whispered, "Why didn't you tell me the truth? Why did you pretend? Why did you let me believe I belonged here?"

The quick answers, the considered explanations, had no effect on the fear that engulfed her.

Her mother had wept.

Her father had said, "But what a terribly cruel thing to do to a child."

Winifred sobbed, "I didn't mean to say it. It just popped out."

And soon, though Mickey didn't remember exactly when, Winifred had gone. But before she left, Mickey had heard her cry defensively, "But I'm your flesh and blood, Benjamin Bassett. It's not right that you should treat me, treat my children, this way. I am your flesh and blood. My children are your flesh and blood." And then, whispering, "And it shows, you know. This child . . . this child has the blood of . . ."

Months of patient love expended, months in the bright dormer room warmed by her parents' concern, lulled Mickey's torment, faded it, buried the fear, and at last drew her back.

Mercifully, she had forgotten most of the details of the breakdown.

But she did remember bits and pieces, small incidents, special days, outings, from the time before.

She and Alexander, pudgy then, too, and arrogant with being older, played on the lawn, while Noah, always rebellious mocked them. Theodora weeping, because Mickey's mother refused to donate diamond earrings for a play. Mickey ran before her father along the canal in spring sunshine. She went to tea at Lord and Taylor's with her mother, both in Easter hats, wearing gloves, and silk dresses, and white shoes. She sat on the front steps, a book on her lap, and Noah wanting to read to her, turned away in white-lipped fury when she refused his help.

Bits and pieces of the childhood somehow shed in Winifred's room.

By the time she was fifteen, she was well. She went away to school, and was rarely home after that. She felt that the weakness that had caused her illness had become her strength when she recovered. Yet Bennett had sensed some hidden doubt in her, had said she must some day go home, resolve that doubt in certainty . . .

Now, she sighed, and turned her back on Winifred's room, and on the memories it evoked.

This was her house. Her home.

She had returned to it to prove to herself that she had outgrown the past.

Yet, as she struggled with her suitcases, climbing the narrow steps to her room, she heard the whispers of the old house, the sigh of the wind in the oak trees outside, the faint hum of a silence deeper than silence.

She banged the suitcases on the floor. The thick carpet muffled the sounds. She pushed open the door, touched the light switch. Lamps became pools of warmth, of invitation, all through the long room, making gleaming mirrors of the big uncurtained windows framed by the cheerful green draperies she had chosen long before.

From one of those windows, the small white-faced girl peered at her with anxious eyes.

Mickey smiled, and the small girl smiled back.

Like twins.

The thought was suddenly there in Mickey's mind.

She grinned, too. She told herself firmly that she was getting as bad as Winifred.

She swung away from the multiple reflections.

There was a lot to do. It was time to begin. Instead, she sat down, took a cigarette without lighting it, and rolled it between her fingers.

In the years while she was away, the breach between the Bassetts and the Warrens had healed, the small unpleasantness with the large consequences, an accidental slip of the tongue, had been forgiven and forgotten, and the Warrens had been kind, helpful, when she and Bennett returned home briefly at her parents' death.

Even so, she was uneasy, hearing nine months later that Winifred intended to visit them in Copenhagen. Bennett said, "She's all the family you have, Mickey." And when Winifred arrived, Mickey was glad to discover that her old fondness for Winifred still remained.

Just a few weeks after Winifred left, Alexander, Noah, and Theodora, traveling in Europe, stopped by for a long weekend.

They had been warm to Mickey, deferential to Bennett. He said, "I never realized, until now, how old I am." He laughed, "With those three in the house, it's like a barrelful of monkeys. Why, this afternoon, Alexander was even writing letters at my desk!" She had apologized for that, for the Warrens' intrusion. But Bennett grinned at her, "Mickey, I'm teasing you! Don't make me feel like a crochety old man."

Alexander said, "We just had to come."

She was relieved when Theodora asked for a list of good shops. She sent Alexander and Theodora off together. But Noah refused to go.

"I didn't come here to go sightseeing or shopping," he told her, smiling.

And later, there were those moments in the garden . . . Noah . . .

A swift sudden shrilling rang in her ears, deafeningly loud in the humming silence. When it stopped, she could hear its echo spread through the empty rooms. When it began again, she identified it, almost laughing in her relief.

She sped down the steps, the narrow flight and the broad one, accompanied by the now familiar on again off again telephone signal. It went silent just as she reached the phone.

She gave a small sigh of disappointment, wondering who could have been calling her. The real estate people? It seemed rather late for that. Winifred? Alexander? Noah?

But there was no use in speculating. She noticed that she had left her hat and purse on the table under the big, gold-framed mirror, and took them, and started back up the steps.

The phone immediately rang again.

She made a run for it, snatched it up, said, "Yes? The Bassett Residence," before she realized the words were on her tongue.

There was no answer.

"Yes," she repeated. "Yes? What number do you want?"

There was still no answer.

She put the phone down, telling herself that some fool had dialed wrong and wouldn't own up to it.

But as soon as she started up the steps, it rang again. She ran back to it, answered, but once more, the only reply was the clear sound of slow breathing. She put the phone down, bewildered, frightened.

She stood there, waiting, to see if another call would come through.

She stood there, listening, listening to the hum of silence in the house.

Suddenly, she noticed that there was something white near the door. She was certain that it hadn't been there earlier.

She went to get it, picked it up, and as she did, the phone rang again.

She grabbed the phone, cried, "Yes? Who is it?" certain that there would be no response. There was none. She hung up without saying any more.

The white thing near the door had been an envelope.

She turned it carefully in her fingers before she slowly opened it.

Inside there was a sheet of paper.

She drew it out, her hands suddenly trembling.

The words were printed carefully in a heavy black ink. They made great black bat tracks across the page.

I know you. But you don't know me.

That's what the bat tracks said.

5

I know you. But you don't know me.

Mickey said the words softly to herself.

They made a kind of sense, but still, she didn't know what they meant.

She studied the envelope. It was plain, unmarked, unaddressed. It must have been slipped under the door some time since the Warrens had left, she realized.

A thick hot wind suddenly seemed to blow through the big hall. The chandelier swayed and whispered, casting moving shadows.

Someone had come into the grounds, crept up on the porch, waited there, listening, then slipped it under the door.

The ringing phone with someone listening to her voice, and not replying . . .

The meaningless note . . .

Quick hot waves of terror engulfed her.

She grabbed her purse, raced up the two flights of steps.

I know who you are. But you don't know me.

Trembling, she heard the strange message in her mind, and then heard the sound of the phone ringing. She stood within the safe and familiar walls of her room, and listened to

60

them, and then the imagined sound became real, no longer imagined. Strident, painful, peal after peal went echoing through the humming silence of the house.

She wanted to run away, to escape into the warm, sweet-scented air of out of doors.

Instead, with the insane ringing in her ears, she set herself to unpack.

In a little while, the few things she had brought with her were placed carefully in the drawers she had used as a young girl. Her dresses and suits were in the closet. Her makeup on the vanity table.

The ringing had stopped at last.

She sat in the chair near the window, rolling an unlit cigarette between her fingers.

Who had left the note under the door? What did it mean?

Who had called her, called her repeatedly, and maintained a suggestive breathing silence when she answered the phone.

She dismissed the real estate people. They had no reason to send her odd notes, or to harass her by phone.

She dismissed Ben Johnson, the cab driver who brought her home.

And who else was there?

The Warrens? Winifred, Theodora, Alexander, Noah?

It was a ridiculous thought.

Why should any one of the Warrens print the note in big black bat tracks, and leave it for her to find when she was alone? Why should they say, *I know you. But you don't know me.* Why should they call her, draw her to the phone, only to offer her silence?

Could it be a prankster? Someone in the neighborhood, who seeing the lights in the house, was teasing her? But again, why? To what purpose would a stranger thrust his unwelcome presence into her home, her consciousness?

She was dizzy with fatigue, with fright. She stayed up as long as she could, watching through the veil of oak leaves beyond her window the occasional flicker of the gaslights at the gate.

But at last, exhausted, she crept into bed.

She was just drifting into uneasy sleep when she heard the strident ring of the phone again.

She buried her head under the pillows, eyes squeezed shut, ears sealed, rigid with fright, waiting, waiting, waiting, until, finally, silence filled the house, and much later, having listened for a long time, she slept.

She awakened with sunshine on her face.

There were mocking birds singing in the oak trees.

The room was filled with the sweet scent of wistaria.

In that instant before remembering, she sat up, smiling. It was a beautiful day. She and Bennett would . . .

And then she knew that she and Bennett would do nothing more together.

She was alone, in Bassett Place.

She listened to the humming silence, and thought of the note she had hidden away in her purse, and waited for the phone to ring, to summon her to that speechless breathing presence again.

But nothing happened.

It was as if she had dreamed, imagined, those moments the night before.

At last, having smoked her first cigarette of the morning, remembering that Bennett always disapproved of her smoking in bed, she got up.

First she went to her purse, looked at the note once more. It was where she had put it, real. She hadn't imagined it, nor dreamed it. Replacing it, she showered and dressed.

She wore a white sleeveless jumper, and low-heeled white buck shoes, and when she brushed her hair she noticed dark circles of exhaustion under her eyes. The extra makeup she used didn't conceal them.

She went downstairs, ignoring the door to Winifred's old room, and switched off the chandelier she had left lit the night before, and with a single quick look at the threshold, she threw the door open.

There was sunlight and blue sky, and the unkempt lawn that rolled down to the tall iron gate.

And there was Noah, pushing himself up from the steps. He gave her a mocking grin. "You sleep late."

"I didn't know you were here," she said.

"I didn't knock. It was so quiet . . ." He stopped. "You should have slept longer by the looks of you."

"I'm fine," she said.

"Aren't you going to invite me in for a cup of coffee?"

She grinned. "Oh, of course."

She gave the threshold near the door a last look. No. There was no note there now.

And the phone was silent, too.

She went ahead of Noah. "Do you want anything besides coffee?"

"I've had breakfast, thanks." He laughed. "I'm not really a member of the leisure classes, Mickey. You just assume that I am."

"What do you mean?"

"I work for a living."

"You do? At what?"

"You know that I paint. Don't you call that work?"

"Yes, of course," she said quickly. "But I thought that . . ."

"You have a common disease. You think painting is something not quite work, and not quite play, don't you?"

"Not really, Noah."

They were in the kitchen by then. He lounged at the table, while she filled a kettle, set it on the stove, busied herself gathering cups and saucers.

Noah grinned at her. "If painting isn't work, and I don't sell, then how do I live?"

She hesitated. "I assumed you had private means. An income of some sort. Like your mother. Like Alexander."

"You're priceless. Did you really think that?"

"As much as I ever thought of it at all," she admitted.

"My dear child, as Winifred would say, my dear Mickey, we, the Warrens, don't have a bean, at least not what you would call a bean. Winifred survives on a tiny trust fund, and credit, hardly enough to keep her in the style she and Theodora are used to. Alexander is ambitious, so he's making good at law. Wills, you know about them, of course, divorces, real estate — Whatever he can turn a hand to. Alexander will probably recoup the Warren fortune one day."

"And you paint," she said, glancing at the steaming kettle.

"I sell a few things here and there. When I get really desperate, I work a couple of months at a time for Alexander. I am a lawyer, too. By training, if not by inclination."

It was hard, Mickey thought, to imagine him as a lawyer. Alexander, plump, and pompous and smiling, always correct, always sedate, seemed right.

But Noah, in wrinkled blue shirt and denim trousers, restlessly shifting his feet, had a lean, sunburned, and sardonic look. She couldn't imagine him having anything at all to do with the law.

He grinned at her. "You realize, of course, that we were all spoiled when young by Bassett largesse. Winifred got used to living high on the hog when she lived here. And that goes for the rest of us, too."

Somehow, suddenly then, she found herself thinking of the note she had found the night before, of the strange and persistent phone calls. A shudder of fear went through her.

He asked, all mockery gone from his voice, "Mickey, what is it? What's wrong?"

"Wrong, Noah?"

"Something has happened, hasn't it? And

you left the hall chandelier on. I could see it burning when I peered inside."

"I just forgot to turn it off," she said calmly, forcing back the impulse to blurt out the truth.

She quickly busied herself pouring coffee, serving him and herself. She didn't dare say, as she was thinking, "I'm afraid. I'm terribly afraid. But I don't know of what, or of whom."

It very nearly happened anyway, for in that instant, her eyes met his, she felt again the strange compelling closeness between them.

But then, he asked, "It's something to do with your coming home, isn't it?"

She sipped coffee to cover her confusion. "I don't know what you mean, Noah."

"It's natural for you to be upset, Mickey." He rose, prowled the kitchen, hands jammed in his pockets. "But why don't you want to talk about it?"

"There's been so little time," she said faintly.

"I'd rather you didn't pretend it has to do with Bennett, Mickey."

She gasped, "Noah, how can you?"

"Ask Winifred," he grinned. "She'll tell you I can do anything." He went on. "It's coming back to this house, isn't it? Coming back to where you found out that you were adopted and got sick with the knowledge."

"I was a child then," she said curtly. "I'm a grown woman now."

"Oh, are you?" he asked, his bottomless dark eyes narrowed, searching, and somehow doubting.

"We all know it was a shock when it happened. But I've had plenty of time to get used to the idea. I was Mother and Father's daughter, truly, even though I wasn't their blood child."

"Of course," Noah said gently. "We all know it. But do you, Mickey?"

She brushed that aside. "Noah, do we have any other family?" She heard the words before she could stop them, and wished she hadn't said them. "Is there anybody else? Besides you and Alexander and Theodora and your mother?"

"No one that I know of." He stared at her. "But why?"

"I wondered."

"It's a funny thing for you to wonder about."

"Is it?" Once again, she covered confusion by sipping her coffee.

I know you. But you don't know me.

Long slow breaths whispering on a telephone wire.

Was there anyone else, anyone besides the Warrens, who could be interested in her? Anyone who could want what she had inherited for instance? Anyone who might hate her?

Noah said, "Why don't you listen to me? Don't stay in this house."

She had always hated any reminder of the myth of her fragility. She had been ill once, but now she was well.

But knowing about the months of her breakdown, knowing she had wept and screamed, and called the house her enemy, he would think that she had come home, and gone mad within the hours of a single night.

So she didn't tell him about the notes, the phone call.

"What does the house mean to you?" he asked.

"It's Bassett Place," she said simply, as if that explained it.

"And you've decided. You're going to stay here."

She repressed a shiver, but nodded.

"Perhaps that's best after all," he said soberly. Then he grinned, cocked his head. "I hear a car. That will be Winifred of course. And maybe Runyon and Bevis. Are you ready for them?"

Mickey jumped to her feet. "Of course. It's sweet of your mother to want to help me."

"She's delighted with the opportunity." He grinned again. "I'll say good-bye now, and take off quickly."

"But why, Noah?"

"It saves stress. She gets upset when she sees me. You'll find out."

But he was too late. There was a knock at the door. It opened, and Winifred called, "Mickey, dear, are you there?"

"Did you want something special?" Mickey asked quickly of Noah.

"To see you." He raised his voice. "We're in the kitchen, Mother."

"In the kitchen? Mickey, dear, I can understand it of Noah. But of you?" Winifred, her words preceding her, surged from the hall, through the other rooms, and into the kitchen. "Have you forgotten how we always lived?" She hugged Mickey, then turned to look at Noah. "How is it that you're up so early?"

"I'm working." Noah nodded at Mickey, said, "I'll be in touch," and went out in the midst of his mother's, "You're working? Ridiculous . . . and the clothes you wear. Noah . . ."

His whistle trailed back. The door closed sharply.

Winifred stopped for breath, sighed, told Mickey, "I believe, really, that he is quite mad." She caught her breath, added hastily, "All artists are, aren't they?" Mickey didn't have to answer. Winifred went on. "Oh, yes, this lovely house . . . And Runyon and Bevis unloading the car. Ready to start, you know . . ."

Runyon.

He was the one to talk to.

Mickey made a dash for the hall.

She met Runyon at the door.

He was small, with a huge head. His hair, once red, was grizzled now to a faded pink. He had big eyes, very warm and very brown, and a huge jaw. He was, in spite of his somewhat misshapen body, very agile. He flung away the bags he was carrying, and opened his arms, crying, "I'm not halfway glad to see you, I'm not."

Mickey kissed him, clung to him. "Oh, Runyon, now I know I'm home."

But when he let her go, and she stepped back, she thought that she had made the same old mistake over again. For Bevis, plump and pink-haired Bevis, was standing there, waiting, a look of pain and hatred on her face.

It had always been that way. Anyone that Runyon loved, Bevis disliked. She wanted her brother for herself, to herself.

But Mickey smiled at her, pecked her cheek, "I'm glad to see you, Bevis."

"So you finally came back," Bevis grumbled. "Well, we'll help you get settled."

Back in the kitchen with Winifred, Mickey

asked, "Can you spare Runyon and Bevis for me? Is it all right, Aunt Winifred?"

"Of course. I know that you're a fragile child. You always were. And after all that you've been through . . . poor Bennett . . . so we must do what we can."

Mickey said, "I'm not a fragile child any more. And I appreciate your help very much."

Winifred ignored that. "Know-how. And money. That's all it takes. And money isn't a problem for you. So you wouldn't understand."

Bevis appeared in the doorway. "We'll start upstairs and work our way down. O.K.?"

Winifred nodded. "Very good, dear."

Bevis backed out, not looking at Mickey.

Winifred said, "I know it's hard to be alone. But remember. You have us. You have your family."

At that moment the phone rang.

"I'll get it," Mickey cried, and hurried into the hall. She caught up the phone on its second ring. She said, "Bassett Place," and waited, knowing exactly what she would hear.

The long slow breaths whispered along the line.

She said softly, "Stop it, do you hear me?" and hung up.

When she had returned to the kitchen, Winifred asked, "Was that Alexander, dear? He said he would call."

"A wrong number."

"Such a nuisance. But as I was saying, you have your family."

And someone else, Mickey thought. Someone who knows me. Someone that I don't know.

"Now," Winifred smiled, her face, as always oddly expressionless, "Shall we have a cup of coffee, and a sit-down and a good chat, while we make our plans?"

6

The plans, the chat, took several hours.

At last, Winifred said, "There," and tucked her gold pencil and her pad into a huge leather bag. "That's enough for now. You're sure about the colors, are you?"

"Oh, yes."

But Mickey wasn't quite sure how the opening of the house had developed into redecorating it, landscaping the lawn. Still, it was a good idea. She was grateful for Winifred's suggestions.

"It shouldn't take too long. Perhaps a month all told," Winifred said. "Perhaps you'd consider staying with us, Mickey?"

Mickey shook her head. "I must stay here." The must was as much for her own benefit as for Winifred.

Winifred gave her a sharp look, hesitated, but then apparently decided not to argue. Instead, she nodded. "I dare say you'll manage fine."

"Of course I will."

Winifred sighed. "It's nice being here like this, with you. Do you remember, when you and Theodora were little, how I used to make dresses for your dolls?"

Mickey nodded. "Always alike. You were fascinated by the idea of twins, weren't you, Aunt Winifred?"

"Was I? I don't suppose so. Not any more than anyone else." But she added, "They are so strange, you know. As if the two truly ought to be one."

At that instant, the phone rang.

"Perhaps that will be Alexander," Winifred said.

When Mickey answered it, expecting nothing but the sound of the empty wire and the usual long slow breaths, it was Alexander, saying, "I hope you'll have dinner with me tonight, Mickey."

Relieved that it was he, instead of her unknown caller, she cried happily, "Oh, I'd love to, Alexander."

He laughed, obviously pleased at her warmth. They set the time, and she hung up. When she returned to the kitchen she told Winifred about the invitation.

"You accepted?" Winifred asked quickly.

"Of course. I'm very pleased."

"Good. I thought you might have other plans."

"I know hardly anyone here."

"Yes, poor dear. That's true. But we'll soon change that. We will have a party for you . . . we'll . . ."

Mickey said firmly, "Aunt Winifred. It's just a month since . . ."

"Why, of course, dear. I realize. I shouldn't have said a party. Just something small. Very informal. For you to meet the people you should meet. After all, dear . . ."

"Not yet."

"Of course. When you're ready, dear. It's entirely up to you." She heaved herself up. "Now, I'll just run along. I do so hate to leave you. But there are some engagements . . ."

"Aunt Winifred, I don't expect you to drop everything just because I've come home, you know."

"Still, I hate for you to be so by yourself. It's just not good for you, I know. You'll brood. You'll think unhealthy thoughts. Dear child, you must not allow that to happen." Winifred's grayish-brown eyes studied Mickey. "You do look drawn this morning."

"Only the trip." Mickey went on, "And I won't brood. I have a lot to do."

But when Winifred had gone, leaving her in the thick warm silence of the empty house, she couldn't think of what she had to do.

Runyon and Bevis continued their cleaning.

Mickey stayed out of their paths, hoping to get Runyon alone for a moment. But Bevis was determined, and remained stubbornly beside Runyon wherever he went.

Mickey decided that her talk with him would have to wait.

It was just after Runyon and Bevis had gone, saying, "Now you're ready for the painters, at least. We'll go back in a few days to see how things go on," that the phone rang.

Mickey made herself go into the hall, made herself pick up the phone, made herself say, "Hello."

Noah laughed. "You don't sound sure you want to talk to anybody."

"Noah!"

"Winifred get you squared away?"

"We've made a lot of plans. And Runyon and Bevis have been and gone. It's a very good start."

"Dinner with me tonight, Mickey?"

"Oh, I'm sorry. Alexander called a little while ago." She hurried on. "But why don't we make it a threesome. He probably didn't realize you'd be available."

"I don't think he'd appreciate my making it a threesome. I'm sure I wouldn't." Then, thoughtfully, "Alexander . . . well, how about tomorrow night, Mickey."

"Good."

"Seven. And be ready." He rang off before she could answer him.

She put down the receiver, smiling.

Bennett had been right. It was good, necessary, to have family.

She was about to go upstairs when she heard a car move up the driveway.

She went to look, saw a florist truck stop at the foot of the steps.

The driver got out, carrying a long white box.

She waited, happily expectant.

"You Marion Mayfield? This Bassett Place?"

She nodded.

He thrust the box at her, said unnecessarily, "Got flowers for you," and went back to the truck.

She watched until he had driven away before she went into the house. She set the screen door latch carefully, and then on the table under the big gold-framed mirror, she opened the box. She gasped at the huge spray thick with purple blossoms. A perfume enveloped her, breathtaking in its strength. She had never seen such flowers before, wondered what they were. She smiled, drew out the small card.

Black ink. Printed words.

I know you. But you don't know me.

She shuddered.

She slammed the cover on the box, huge spray still inside. Then, suddenly, she thought of the florist shop. She checked the box. Yes. The address was there.

Ben Johnson's card was still in her purse, along with the note she had received the night before.

She put on a small white hat, found gloves, and went downstairs. She dialed the number on Ben's card, waited impatiently at the busy signal, then dialed again. That time she got through. She asked for the driver named Ben Johnson, and was told he was just a few blocks from her house, would be there in a little while.

She carefully locked the back door, re-checked the windows, locked the front door after her. Then, remembering, she went inside again to get the big white box.

She was at the foot of the steps waiting when the cab pulled in.

Ben smiled widely. "I never thought you'd call me. You get settled all right last night?"

"Just fine," she told him. And getting in, she gave him the name of the florist shop, the address.

"In Georgetown. Won't take us long to get there." He pulled away. Then, with a curious dark eye in the mirror, asked, "You decide you don't want them flowers?"

She hesitated, but finally said, "I want to find out who sent them."

"They leave out the card?"

"There's a card. But no name."

He chuckled, "Some secret admirer of yours, welcoming you back, I reckon."

She hesitated again, wishing she hadn't said anything. It was simply too hard to explain. The note, the phone calls, now the flowers. It sounded . . . it sounded crazy. She must wait, talk to Runyon, ask him what to do. At last, she said vaguely, "That might be it. But I'm curious."

In a little while, he parked at the florist. "I'll wait if you want."

She thanked him, went inside.

The sweet, almost fetid scent of the flowers choked her. An elderly man, sitting on a high stool behind the counter, put aside the newspaper he had been reading, and looked at her.

"I received these flowers this morning," she said, opening the box. "Can you tell me who sent them?"

"You mean I forgot to put the card in? That's bad. What's a man coming to if he can't even remember to put a card in?"

She said hastily, "There's a note. But no name. I thought you might have a record of . . ."

"No name. But a note. Then I didn't forget, did I?" He smiled his relief. "Well, that's good. Let's see. Oh, yes . . . the twinberry.

I remember that. Asked for it special. We don't get too many calls. She . . ." He paused, peered at Mickey through his rimless glasses. "Listen, is this some kind of a joke? I'm an old man. And I'm past jokes. If you youngsters don't have more to do than bother . . ."

"It's not a joke. Do you know who sent them?"

"That's what I mean," he retorted irritably. "The twinberry, yes. She . . . That's it. You're the girl, aren't you?"

"I?" Mickey demanded.

"I can see now, probably you're not. But still, maybe you are."

"A girl ordered them?" Mickey demanded, trying to make sense out of what he was saying. "And she looks like me?"

He nodded, reached for his newspaper. "That's all I know."

"You mean she's about my height, coloring, age?"

He grunted. "That's what I mean."

"But it wasn't me," Mickey insisted.

"Maybe not. I didn't study her."

"When was she here?"

"This morning. About two minutes after I opened up. And she paid cash, and went out. That was that. I ordered them from the supplier and shipped them out to you."

"And you don't know her name?"

He shrugged, didn't bother to answer.

Mickey turned away from the counter.

"Well, take your flowers. They're paid for."

"I don't want them," she said in a thin whisper.

"You find out anything?" Ben Johnson asked, when she got into the cab.

"Yes. It was twinberry."

"Twinberry? I know that. It's a kind of honeysuckle, isn't it?" He grinned at her in the rear view mirror. "Funny thing to send for a surprise."

Twinberry, Mickey thought.

Winifred. Could Winifred have left the note the night before? Could Winifred have gotten someone to send her the flowers? But why? Why?

But no . . . a phone call had come while Winifred sat in the kitchen.

Mickey pressed her hands to her head.

Noah then? Of course not. It couldn't have been Noah.

Then what of Alexander?

Or Theodora?

No. It was ridiculous. They were all family.

I know you. But you don't know me.

Some stranger then. A nameless, faceless person, who for reasons known only to herself, wanted to torment Mickey, to drive her . . .

She stopped the thought still born. She would not be driven. Not in any way.

Ben turned in the gate under the flickering gaslights. "Always burning," he said.

"Always," she answered. "As long as Bassett Place stands."

They sat side by side on a plush-covered bench in a small alcove. Mirrors made walls on three sides of them.

Multiple images of herself and Alexander flashed at her. She tried to ignore them.

"You know," Alexander said, leaning close to her, "I always knew, even when we were small, that you would grow up to be beautiful."

"Did you?" Mickey laughed. "I don't see how you could have. I was all big eyes and sticking-out bones. And . . ." she added, "I haven't changed much since."

"You've changed. Though you could do with a bit more flesh on those bones," he grinned. "Now that we've got you home, we'll see to that." He went on, "But then, I'm afraid I was fat, mean-tempered, and a terrible tease. I hope you've forgiven me for that, Mickey. It was only because I was so charmed by you."

"It seems hardly possible, Alexander," she laughed.

"Little boys will be little boys." His full face was pink, well-shaven, his eyes very blue and bright. He went on, "I'm sure you don't realize it, but when I saw you again in Copenhagen, saw you again, Mickey, I wished it had all been different. You . . . our family . . . it seems so wrong that we should have been alienated."

"But we weren't, Alexander. Not really."

"All those years . . ."

She said gently, "I was away at school. And, of course, after I married Bennett . . ."

"But we ought to have kept in touch more. We were very wrong, all of us. We . . . I, at least, will make it up to you, Mickey."

She smiled at him. "You already have."

In that moment of warmth, she thought of telling him about the note, the phone calls, the flowers.

"We want to take care of you, Mickey."

Something, a special timbre in his voice, perhaps, told her that he was thinking of her breakdown.

No, she told herself. She mustn't tell Alexander, nor any of the Warrens.

Runyon. Runyon would advise her.

She said, "Alexander, Bennett left all my father's papers with you, didn't he?"

"Yes, he did. It seemed wisest. And you

needn't worry. I'll handle them for you. Bennett's instructions, desires, are extremely clear. He might well have been a lawyer himself."

"I'd like to go through everything, Alexander, to familiarize myself with my holdings."

"Go through everything? What on earth for, Mickey?"

"Just so that I know what's there."

"Bennett trusted my judgment enough to leave things in my hands. Don't you think you can do the same?"

"Of course," she said hastily. "But I still would like to understand better what I have. You'll continue to handle it all for me, if you're willing to, that is."

"Why worry your pretty little head? You should be enjoying yourself, thinking of your future. What difference do your father's papers, or Bennett's, for that matter, make to you?"

She said slowly, "All my life people have taken care of things for me, Alexander. First my father, then Bennett. And now . . . well, now I want to . . . take care of myself."

"I see." Alexander smiled. "Well, you just name the day." He half rose. "That sounds like a good tune. Wouldn't you like to dance?"

She hesitated.

"Mickey, you can't really believe that Bennett would object."

She moved with Alexander to the dance floor.

Bennett had not believed in mourning clothes, nor in mourning periods. Then she must not mourn.

7

There was a great clatter below.

Mickey quickly sketched a pink mouth on her lips, and hurried downstairs.

The painting crew had obviously arrived.

She wasn't sure of exactly what she must do. But when she opened the door to the five men, she discovered that she herself had nothing to do.

They brushed by her, grinning quick good mornings, and hauling tarpaulins and paint brushes and ladders with them.

She said vaguely, "I suppose you know where to begin?"

The foreman told her, "I've got all the directions. Mrs. Warren wrote them down."

Mickey, relieved, went into the kitchen.

She was drinking her breakfast coffee when Winifred arrived, perfectly coiffed, and made up, more of the *grande dame* than ever.

Winifred's voice, the clatter and shouts and laughter from the third floor, brought unexpected life to the quiet house.

The odd note, the phone calls, the flowers, seemed to be no more than a dream.

Winifred, settling across the table from

Mickey, coffee cup in hand, said, "I'm delighted to see that the painters are on time. Difficult to schedule them so quickly." She shrugged. "But of course, an expensive firm. With enough money, you can do anything." She was, meanwhile, fishing around in her big bag. She murmured, "Now where did I put it?" and then murmured a triumphant, "Ah, here," and brought out a newspaper clipping. "You might not have seen this, Mickey. It was in the morning papers the day you arrived."

Mickey accepted the newspaper clipping, read it, at first startled, and then somewhat embarrassed. The headline said, MARION BASSETT MAYFIELD RETURNS. The article went on, "Marion (Mickey) Bassett Mayfield, heir to the Bassett fortune, widow of the late Mr. Bennett Mayfield, has returned to Bassett Place on Palisade Heights for an indefinite stay."

"But how did they know?" Mickey asked finally.

"I phoned it in," Winifred retorted. "How else, my dear? As soon as the real estate people called Alexander, and he called me . . ."

"But, Aunt Winifred, why?"

"Mickey, dear, the Bassetts are important people in Washington. Do try to understand that. Oh, I realize that Benjamin and your mother played humble because it suited them to. But people are interested. And if you're to take your place in the right circles . . ."

"The day I arrived?" Mickey said thoughtfully.

"That very morning. As a matter of fact, you weren't even here yet. And it took some doing," Winifred answered smugly. "If I hadn't known just who to speak to, just what to say . . ."

But Mickey, no longer listening, thought that with the item in the paper, anyone interested, anyone who cared, would have known.

The note, the calls, the flowers, became real again.

Mickey shivered.

Winifred went on, "There was something in, I suppose I still have the clipping around, when you and Bennett were here before. After your parents' funeral, I mean. You probably didn't see it. I'll try to find it for you."

"It doesn't matter," Mickey managed to say.

Winifred changed the subject. "I hope you're certain about the colors we chose. It will soon be too late. You must be more than acquiescent, you know. You must be pleased."

"I am pleased," Mickey said, thinking that Winifred knew a great deal more about such things than she herself did. It was not only easier to defer, it would produce a more successful result.

"Such a lovely house," Winifred told her. "Belonging to the Bassetts, built by them, for them. It must be right, you know."

"Of course," Mickey agreed, wondering just when, how, she had decided that she would keep the house. She had originally planned to stay there only until she had made some firm decision. It appeared that the decision had been made some time the day before, more easily than she would have expected.

She smiled fondly at Winifred.

"And since you have the money, you must have the best. I can't tell you, dear, what a difference that makes in how one lives. You can't imagine. You don't know. You never will."

She paused. A small silence fell.

The laughter, the footsteps, the banging sounds from upstairs suddenly seemed very loud.

Was Winifred hinting? Mickey asked herself.

Noah had said that Winifred's trust fund was very small, inadequate for Winifred's and Theodora's needs and tastes. Was Winifred hoping that Mickey would make some settlement on her?

Winifred, smoothing the piled-high white waves, suddenly smiled. "Mickey, my dear, I realize that I, so much older than you, so experienced, must seem to be taking the reins. But you must understand, dear. I just want to help, to make things easier for you."

"It's very kind of you," Mickey said reassuringly.

"But you are so quiet, so without . . . so without enthusiasm . . . one doesn't want to inflict . . ."

"I'm afraid I'm tired this morning, Aunt Winifred."

There had been no calls the night before.

But she had lain awake after Alexander brought her home.

She had been waiting for the phone to ring.

Winifred said, "But you are well? You must be sure not to overtax yourself, you know. You never were a strong child. I always told Benjamin that." Winifred stopped herself. "So much has happened, too."

"A lot has," Mickey agreed, annoyed that once again the myth of her fragility had been stressed. "But I'm as strong as a horse. It's just that my evening with Alexander ended late."

"It was pleasant then?"

"Oh, yes."

"He is a pleasant person to be with, if I

do say so myself," Winifred said. "You do find him so?"

The odd modulation of her voice, uneven as always, stressed some words, understressed others, implying a mysterious double meaning.

Mickey agreed.

"Restful, protective, solid, don't you think?"

Again, Mickey agreed.

"A strong shoulder to lean upon. For me. And I hope you will find him the same for you. You will, I know, if you want to." Winifred smiled again. "Of course, it's no secret to you, Mickey. Alexander adores you, and always has."

Mickey gave her a blank look.

Adore seemed to be rather a strong word.

Winifred drew on her gloves. "Now then, dear, we must be on our way. You're ready, aren't you?"

"Ready?" Mickey echoed.

"For our shopping trip." Winifred asked sharply, "Dear, you do remember. We were to go into Georgetown today. We must get started on the upholstery fabric, the rugs, immediately. There's a great deal to do. We decided yesterday."

Mickey jumped up. "Oh, of course. I'll just get a purse."

"And a hat," Winifred murmured. "You do have a hat."

Mickey grinned. "Yes. Plenty of hats."

She chose a pink straw that matched her linen suit.

She stopped to redo her lips.

Over-large gray eyes regarded her soberly from the mirror.

Mickey dutifully followed Winifred from one Georgetown shop to another.

They passed the florist where Mickey had gone the day before. Through the big front window, she caught a glimpse of the elderly man she had spoken to then. He was still reading his newspaper.

In the bright hot sun of August, with Winifred chatting beside her, and the crowds of people around her, her fear while speaking to him seemed no more than a nightmare out of distant childhood.

There had been no more notes, no more calls.

Perhaps the game was over.

It was a pleasant, busy, fruitful day.

Mickey, finally exhausted, though Winifred seemed as fresh as in the morning, was relieved to part from Winifred.

She took a cab back to the house.

As she crossed the threshold, she thought

she heard whispering voices. She wavered there, suddenly cold in the summer heat.

It was a brief moment, but to her it seemed endless.

A burst of laughter reminded her that the painters were in the house.

She told herself that she must get over her odd reaction to Bassett Place. It was her home, and she loved it, and . . . and yes, she would live there happily and safely.

She took off her hat before the sparkling mirror.

The phone rang.

Her hand shook as she picked up the receiver. Her voice shook as she said hello.

It was Noah asking, "Seven still all right?"

"Of course. Why?"

He hesitated. "I just spoke to Winifred. She seemed to think you were in a state of collapse. And you do sound . . ."

Mickey forced a laugh. "I shopped with Winifred for most of the day."

"That explains it." There was another pause. "But, in fact, you do sound odd, Mickey."

"I've just come in the door."

He chuckled. "I should have known better than to listen to Winifred. See you at seven."

Mickey said good-bye and hung up. Her

hand was still on the receiver when the phone rang again.

She picked it up, thinking that Noah had called her back for some reason. She said, "Noah?"

There was no answer.

Through the humming silence she heard long slow breaths . . . long slow menacing breaths.

She listened for a moment, then slammed the receiver down.

So the game was not over.

She found the phone directory, got the number, and called service. She explained the problem first to one young-sounding, sympathetic voice, then to an old-sounding, sympathetic voice, then, finally, to one ageless, tired, and not sympathetic at all, who said, "Yes, yes. It's a problem we do have. But you do understand? There's really nothing to worry about. Such people are perfectly harmless. They expend their energy doing just what they are doing to you. But it's only for a few days so far. We can't go on that. Wait a week or two. Usually they get tired of it. But if it continues, call us back. We'll see then."

It was obvious that the ageless, tired, not at all sympathetic one didn't think that there was much he could do. And didn't care. And probably, Mickey thought, he was right that such people were harmless. But still, he didn't know about the note, the flowers.

The painters finished for the day and left. The house was still.

It breathed gently, and watched, and whispered.

Mickey told herself not to be ridiculous, but she shivered as she went upstairs to bathe and dress.

She wore red, a sharp, joyful, defiant red, a dress with a tiny waist, and full flaring skirt.

Noah grinned at her, with a speculative twist of his mouth, dark eyes full of the usual mockery. "Very pretty. All for me? You could be a carnation."

Somehow she wished that he hadn't mentioned flowers.

"Where are we going?" she asked.

"To dinner first. Where there's a view. And then . . ." He shrugged. "Let's see how it goes, shall we?"

The view was from the roof of a downtown hotel.

The gleaming white stalk of the Washington Monument seemed close enough to touch. Hazy air made halos around street lights strung like pearls along the wide avenues. The Capitol dome seemed to float against a backdrop of deep, starry blue.

Mickey sipped her drink contentedly, and admired the city below.

"You still seem a sleeping princess to me," Noah said suddenly.

She turned, surprised, "Do I?"

"Of course. And don't you remember?"

She did remember.

His words took her back to the garden in Copenhagen. She had been gathering flowers, and Noah walked beside her. Noah . . . the skeptical twist in his mouth, the burning black eyes full of mockery. He walked beside her, and for no reason that she knew, in response to nothing that she understood, said, "You're like a sleeping princess, Mickey. When are you going to wake up?"

Now she laughed softly. "I remember, Noah."

"I still wonder."

"But I am awake, Noah."

"No. You're waiting for something. Don't you know that?"

"Waiting for something?" she repeated uncomfortably.

"To find someone, perhaps," he went on in a sober voice. "Or is it to find yourself?"

She echoed him again. "To find myself?"

He asked softly, "Mickey, why are you frightened?"

"I don't know what you mean."

"Don't you?" The mocking light was suddenly in his narrowed eyes. "You have been. Ever since you came home. And now more than ever."

Why, she asked herself suddenly, did he insist on probing, on questioning her?

She shook her head, set her lips.

He said gently, "Is there no one, no one in this world now, that you can trust, Mickey?"

She thought wildly, but who can I trust? I don't know what's happening. I don't know why. I can't even trust myself.

Noah had called her earlier, found her at home. Only moments later the phone had rung again.

Could he, bitter at having been raised as a rich man's son, with none of the substance to enjoy the life for which he had been prepared, actually hate her?

Bennett had said that coincidences happened. He must be right. But still, she had a feeling about coincidences. And the two calls had come so close together . . .

And Winifred, sighing, saying that Mickey would never have to worry about money. Was that a hint? Was that an indication that Winifred wanted, hoped, in some way, to get the Bassett fortune? Did she hate Mickey because Mickey, adopted by the Bassetts, had inherited what Winifred thought should belong to her and to her children?

Or Alexander . . . why had he seemed to resent her desire to look through her father's papers? To familiarize herself with what was hers? Was there something among those papers that Alexander didn't want her to see? But he was obviously successful himself, working at something he liked, with a fine future before him.

What about Theodora, plump, pretty Theodora, who was interested only in clothes, good times, in the things that it took money to buy.

And, Mickey asked, was she, herself, to be trusted? Were her own senses, emotions, safe? Why had she been so frightened when the elderly florist mentioned twinberry as the spray he had sent her. Why, knowing she hadn't ordered them, had it upset her so to think that he confused her with the girl that had?

A plane swooped low, searchlight reaching ahead, green and red landing lights blinking, signalling.

Noah said, "You could be fooled into thinking that you could reach out and touch it, couldn't you? That's what illusion does."

Illusion, Mickey thought. There was the explanation. From the moment of her arrival at the house, she had allowed herself to be trapped in a web of illusion.

She walked in the long and living shadow of the past.

She shivered.

"It's not very easy to grow up," Noah said.

She folded her hands carefully in her lap. She made herself smile at him. "I don't know what you're talking about," she answered.

They stopped for a drink at his apartment. "So you can see how I live," he told her. "Winifred and Alexander have their place together, and Theodora with them, as you know. But me . . ." he shrugged. "I prefer to go it alone."

It was three rooms, brightly clean, pleasant, and with nothing of that off-beat quality that Noah himself had led her to expect. His studio was cluttered, but obviously a serious workroom. It was in his paintings that she saw reflected the mockery so often in his deep dark eyes.

She said, "You love your work, don't you?"

"That's why I do it."

"Money . . . it doesn't mean a thing to you, Noah."

He laughed. "All right. You know my secret now." He went on, suddenly sober. "I wish I knew yours, Mickey."

8

"It's lovely to be here like this," Winifred said, leaning back, so that the smooth white waves of her piled-high hair gleamed in the candlelight. "All of us together in Bassett Place. Just as we used to be."

"Lovely," Theodora murmured, her plump face full of satisfaction, her plump hand moving to her throat to touch the strand of pearls Mickey had given her.

Mickey was no more certain of how it was that she had made the gift of those pearls to Theodora than she was certain of how it had come about that the Warrens returned to Bassett Place.

She remembered thinking that she must decide what to do about the house. She had been going to stay there, until her decision was made. She remembered that Winifred told her the night of her arrival that she, the children, would move in with her to keep her from being alone. Mickey had been noncommittal about that, she was sure. She didn't remember coming to a conscious decision about keeping the house. Overnight, she and Winifred began the planning. Painters arrived. And some time during the redecorating, Winifred chose colors for her room, and Theodora's and Alexander's.

Mickey's reaction to the arrangement was mixed. She supposed that she had been inadequate to deal with Winifred's blend of solicitude and proprietary sense so well seasoned with a youthful wistfulness. To have refused, if there had ever been a moment when it could have been refused, Winifred's gently offered care and companionship, would have required more blatant resistance than Mickey could summon. But she was relieved that having chosen to keep Bassett Place and live in it, she would not have to face staying there alone. And Bennett, she was certain, would have approved.

Only Noah, openly mocking, did not. "That's a ridiculous arrangement," he told her. "And I thought you said you were all grown up, Mickey."

"It seems wise to me," she said.

"It isn't." He refused to give his reasons for saying that, just as he refused, in spite of Winifred's pressure, to rejoin the family. "No, thank you," he growled at his mother. "I'm no Bassett."

"But you are," she retorted. "You're directly, genetically, related to Benjamin Bassett himself. You're more a Bassett than . . ."

Winifred stopped then.

But Mickey finished the sentence in her own mind. "You're more a Bassett than Mickey is."

She couldn't resent what was nothing but the truth. It might hurt. Yes, somehow even then, the truth could still hurt. But she couldn't deny it.

It didn't matter that the Bassetts had told her, "Mickey, we've had you since two days after you were born. You are ours, ours. You belong here, with us, to us."

They had also told her, when she insisted on knowing, that her true mother had been young, beautiful, married to a soldier killed in the Italian campaign. Her mother had wanted to keep her, but alone, with no one to help, she finally agreed to allow Mickey to be adopted. Within a few days after that, the young, beautiful girl died of post-delivery complications.

That was all Mickey knew. Since recovering from her illness, she had been satisfied with her parents' explanations. Her acceptance, she knew, was one sign that her recovery was, in fact, complete. She had been completely well for years, the nightmare months wiped out. Yet there had lingered within her some small seed of doubt. Having once crossed the line between reality and nightmare, could she ever cross it again? Bennett had sensed that doubt. And she, returning to the house, once again engulfed by the familiar fear, hearing the whispers, sensing the watching eyes, was forced to accept it, to live with it, until she had learned to resolve it.

She felt, too often, as if she were a stranger, an intruder in a life where she didn't belong.

And, within the first few hours of her return, the whispering voice had developed words.

I know you. But you don't know me.

The voice had developed a faint shape, that of a girl seen by an elderly florist.

Then the note on the threshold, that first night, after the calls, the spray of twinberry, that first day, after that single call on the second day, the whispering voice had lost its words, the faint shape of the voice had faded.

The game ended as abruptly as it had begun.

Bewildered, but relieved, Mickey wondered why.

Perhaps it was because it was so obvious that she was not alone. Perhaps because a game that led nowhere must quickly lose its pleasure. She supposed that she would never really know.

"It is lovely, isn't it?" Winifred was saying so insistently that Mickey knew the question was a repetition.

"You've done a beautiful job, Aunt Winifred," she said quickly. "Truly, I don't know how you managed it."

Winifred's grayish-brown eyes brightened with pleasure, but she shrugged, "Why, it was nothing, Mickey. A joy for me." She went on, "And I am delighted to see that you're back with us."

"Back with you?"

Winifred laughed softly, her expressionless face as empty as always. "My dear, you do tend to drift off. Woolgather, daydream. I don't know just what to call it. But really, dear . . ."

"I was thinking," Mickey said. "Admiring the draperies. They were such a good idea."

"And the proper background for you," Alexander put in, admiring her, rather than the window hangings. "But you seemed to be thinking such long long thoughts, Mickey."

She was glad that she had never told the Warrens about the odd things that happened when she first returned to the house. Even without that knowledge, they so plainly suspected her of some continuing instability, so plainly watched her, concerned lest the old illness had left its mark on her. That, she admitted to herself, irritated her out of proportion to its importance. She had, in the week since they moved in, reminded herself many times that their attitude was understandable, but she still didn't like it, and was relieved that she hadn't given them any reason for even greater concern.

Though she had thought, in her terror, to tell Runyon about it, the opportunity had simply not arisen. He and Bevis worked together, like four arms on one body. And it was to Runyon alone that Mickey had wanted to talk. But now, since the silly, frightening game was ended, she supposed that it was just as well that she had said nothing about it.

"With everything just right," Winifred was saying, "we must begin to think of a small party, a housewarming, a . . ."

It was one of those times when Mickey wished, in spite of Bennett's feelings, that she had chosen to wear mourning. It would remind Winifred and everyone else that Mickey had been widowed just two months before. But she said gently, "I think it's too soon, Aunt Winifred."

"Whatever you say, my dear. We'll wait until you feel ready. But life does go on. And Bennett, I am sure, would not want . . ."

Mickey supposed that there would soon be a housewarming, however. For she had learned that no matter how much Winifred deferred to her, Winifred always had her own way in the end.

It had been that way over the ivory draperies that hung at the dining room windows, that way over the moss green rug.

Winifred's unguessable age, her formidable spirit, her oddly modulated words, were the gears of an unstoppable steamroller.

Frowning, Winifred said, "You mustn't brood, dear child. I hope all this wasn't too much for you. You do look tired, terribly tired."

"You did it all," Mickey smiled.

"I only wanted to help."

"You helped so much, Aunt Winifred."

Winifred shrugged. "When you have money, dear . . . it's easy. Anything is easy."

Was that another hint? Mickey asked herself. Was she being told, indirectly, that she, an outsider, an adopted child, had no real right to the Bassett fortune?

"Oh, I do so wish that Noah weren't so stubborn, so selfish. If only he were with us now."

Alexander laughed, his pudgy face flushed in the candlelight. "It's his loss." He looked meaningfully at Mickey. "I hope you're not offended, nor regretful, that he refused your kind offer, Mickey."

She wondered why Alexander sounded so pompous. He was only thirty years old. Bennett, at fifty-five, had seemed younger, except, and she almost smiled then, when he

107

was lecturing her.

She managed a smile for Alexander. "Noah must do what he wants, you know."

"Which is to tumble in and out of here at all hours of the days or night, but not to settle down like a sensible person," Winifred grumbled.

"Oh, it's not as bad as all that," Mickey protested.

"Bevis and Runyon adore him, of course," Winifred said. "But just the same, not knowing if there'll be four or five, for meals . . . it is rather . . . well, a bore, for us, and a nuisance for them."

Mickey stifled a yawn. To change the subject, she said to Alexander, "You know, you never did bring home father's papers for me to start on. You did say that they are in your safe, didn't you?"

"Oh, yes. That's where they are all right."

"Then I would like to see them, Alexander."

"Of course, Mickey. I'll bring them home tomorrow."

She wondered if he remembered that he had already twice promised her that, and twice not followed through.

"Though I can't see why you want to trouble your pretty little head with all that, Mickey," he went on.

"It's something I feel I should do, Alexander. Bennett handled everything for me for so long . . ." She stopped. Sudden tears stung her eyes.

Bennett had done everything for her . . . everything, everything . . .

She had been the protected child, he the loving father.

No wonder she had never guessed that he was ill.

Her blindness had resulted from the nature of their marriage.

Alexander was saying, "And Bennett turned it over to me, Mickey."

"Of course," she agreed. "But you will bring the papers home tomorrow, won't you?" There was a certain tartness in her voice.

She knew that Alexander heard it, for he answered, blue eyes narrowing, "I said I would, Mickey."

The sound of the phone interrupted what threatened to be a too long silence.

Runyon put his pink head in the doorway. "Alexander?" he growled. "Telephone for you," and disappeared.

Alexander got up, quickly went into the hall.

Mickey, wanting a cigarette, rose, too.

"Where are you going?" Theodora asked, and when Mickey explained, said, "I'll get them."

But Mickey, already on her feet, thanked Theodora, and went into the living room, amused that plump Theodora, usually so lazy, should suddenly want to be helpful.

Collecting her cigarettes, pausing to light one, Mickey heard Alexander, voice lowered, but still audible.

"Look, don't call me here. I told you not to." He stopped, obviously listening, then went on, "I can't help that. Just do what I say. It's important."

Mickey returned to the dining room.

Bevis had served the coffee in her absence.

Stirring it absently, Mickey wondered why Alexander didn't want someone to call him at the house. She supposed that it had something to do with a case. Perhaps he felt the need to separate his office from his home.

When he came back, his thick shoulders hunched irritably, he said, "I'm sorry. Some of my clients . . ."

"The problems of success," Theodora told him, grinning.

Alexander began to describe a case of his in great detail. He loved to go on at length, presuming everyone was as interested in law as he was.

Mickey stifled another yawn, and thought about Noah.

When the meal was over, Winifred, with

many apologies, announced that it was her bridge night.

Theodora hurried off to ready herself for a date.

Alexander told Mickey, "There's a new place in Georgetown — The Spinning Wheel."

"Is there?"

"Let's see what it's like."

"I think not, Alexander. Not tonight," she said.

Winifred cried, "But my dear child, I never dreamed you intended to stay at home. I do so dislike to leave you alone."

"That's all right," Mickey said, smiling. "I am a bit old for a nursemaid."

"A nursemaid?" Winifred frowned. "Why, dear child, I didn't intend to imply any such thing. But do, to please me, just go along with Alexander."

But Mickey was adamant. Their insistence was wearing, yet she refused to change her mind.

She had realized, thinking of Bennett, of the nature of their marriage, that she had been treated as a child because she had encouraged it. The Warrens would treat her the same way unless she showed them quickly that she was an adult, and would not allow them to pamper her.

Finally, sighing, Winifred departed.

Alexander gave in then, too.

Mickey, finally alone, had a second cup of coffee, and chatted with Runyon, and then went up to her room.

It had been redone, was clean and bright. But somehow it looked the same as before. The walls were still white, the heavy drapes at the big windows a deep forest green that exactly matched the thick green rug.

The late September wind was cool on her face, ruffled her black curls.

She lit a cigarette, took a book, and sat down to read.

A little later, she heard a door below close. She knew that Runyon and Bevis were going back to their apartment over the garage, as they did every evening when the work in the house was finished.

She was alone, completely alone.

She closed the book, leaned her head against the chair back, listening. She sat that way for one helpless moment, and then she jumped to her feet.

She told herself that there were no whispering voices in the house. She must not listen for them. There were no watching eyes in the house. She must not look for them.

The phone rang. She looked at the extension that had been installed in her room, in Winifred's room, in the apartment over the garage.

Runyon would answer it first, saying in his deep growl, "Bassett Place." If the call were for her, he would push a certain button, and . . .

She heard the faint ting that was the signal. She took up the receiver, answered.

The familiar, the too familiar long slow breaths came across the empty line.

Long, slow breaths that instantly made her dizzy with terror.

She hung up. Her hand shook as she touched the button that would signal Runyon.

He answered, "Were you calling us, Mickey? Or is that a mistake? These new gadgets never work. I halfway knew . . ."

Mickey cut in, "Runyon, was there a call for me just now?"

"Yes. Yes, there was. Why? Were you . . ."

She cut in again. "Can Bevis hear you, Runyon?"

"No. She's inside, watching the teevee. What's this all about? Were you disconnected?"

"Not exactly. But I wondered . . . do you know who it was calling? Was it a man or a woman? How did they ask for me?"

There was a brief moment of silence.

Runyon was considering, Mickey knew, and suddenly wished that she hadn't asked all those questions.

At last, he said, "I'm coming over."

"No . . . it's not . . ."

"I'll be there in a minute." He hung up.

She could imagine him snatching up his dark coat, pulling it on, to hide the slight hump in his shoulders.

She had been dizzy with terror listening to the long slow breaths on the empty line. Now she was almost dizzy with relief listening for the sound of his footsteps.

She hurried downstairs to meet him in the kitchen.

He came in, pink hair ruffled, demanding before he was past the threshold, "Now what's all this, Mickey?" and adding, "I don't know who it was. Don't you know? Somebody just said, 'Mrs. Mayfield.' That's you. A whispery kind of voice. Now why?"

She remembered that she had been glad she hadn't told him about the odd frightening game that had tormented her those first few days after she returned home. But that was when she thought the game was over.

She sat down, braced her trembling legs, said, "I don't know what to do, Runyon."

He took a chair across from her. He massaged his huge jaw, his brown eyes fixed on her face. "Tell me what it's all about, Mickey."

She explained as quickly as she could. She told him about the first night, the phone calls, the note, about the first day, the calls, the huge spray of twinberry with the second note, about the second day, the phone call. "That finished it," she said at last. "I thought that finished it, Runyon."

He regarded her thoughtfully, still massaging his big jaw. "I don't halfway like it. You still have those notes?" At her nod, he went on, "I'd like to see them, Mickey."

She went up to her room.

A whispery voice, Runyon had said.

A whispery voice like the whispers in the house.

She found the notes in the bookcase where she had hidden them. She brought them down to Runyon.

He read them slowly, examined each sheet of white paper. He shook his pink head. " 'I know you. But you don't know me.' Now that doesn't make much sense, does it?"

"I don't know."

His deep growl softened. "Now wait a minute, Mickey. Don't look . . . don't look like that. I'll find out, and I'll stop it. You haven't got a thing to worry about. Runyon will take care of it for you." He braced his misshapen body as he rose. "You let me think a little. Then we'll see."

"I never told the Warrens," she said.

"Should have. Ought to have done something. Told somebody. But it's going to be O.K. now."

But when he left her, the warmth of his reassurance went with him.

She went up to her room, fear prickling through her.

I know you. But you don't know me.

Black print on white paper.

Twinberry.

Long, slow breaths on an empty line.

And had she, looking so hard into his brown eyes, seen a question there?

Had he, studying the notes, wondered if she had written them? Written them to herself? Had he wondered if she was standing once again at the entrance to the valley of the long and living shadow?

She jumped to her feet.

She wanted to run away.

But where? How?

And this was her home. She knew that if she left, she would be destroyed forever.

From below, there came the peal of the door bell.

She tripped and stumbled, hurrying to get down the steps. She flung the door open, braced, ready for anything, she told herself.

But Noah grinned at her. "Why were you running? I came to see you. I wasn't going to leave." And then, no longer grinning,

"Mickey, what's the matter?"

She threw herself into his arms, sobbing, "Oh, I'm so glad it's you."

He held her close, stroked her hair. "Tell me, Mickey."

But she, startled and shocked by her response to his touch, drew away . . . those moments in the Copenhagen garden . . . his smile . . . and Bennett, Bennett . . .

She said finally, "It's nothing, Noah."

He studied her, his bottomless dark eyes thoughtful, but instead of questioning her further, he asked, "What about a ride?"

Escape from the house, even for a little while, appealed to her. She took a sweater, followed him to his car.

They drove for a long while without speaking.

The humming tires, the relaxed silence, lulled her into a pleasant reverie, her fear, her questions, forgotten.

But finally Noah said, "Won't you tell me what's bothering you, Mickey?" and smiling at her, "Not that I mind your throwing yourself into my arms. Please don't think that. But I know you were scared. I want to know why."

She shook her head. She had told Runyon. He would help her. She couldn't tell Noah, too. "I was . . . I was just glad to see you, Noah."

"Obviously. But why?"

Her cheeks burned. She didn't answer him.

He slid her a mocking look. "This is so sudden, you know."

"Noah, stop it," she cried.

"I thought I'd make you smile."

"Never mind."

"But you still haven't smiled."

The night air cooled her burning cheeks. The pulses in her throat gradually slowed. They talked of casual things. By the time Noah brought her back to the house, she felt ready to face it. She did smile, and he noticed it as they drove past the dancing gaslights at the iron gates.

"Much better," he grinned. "We'll have to do this again."

"Yes," she agreed. "Much better."

But Alexander was on the porch, pudgy, thick-shouldered, and oddly menacing. "I thought you wanted to stay home," he told Mickey.

"Noah dropped by. A ride seemed a good idea."

"Noah dropped by," Alexander repeated ominously. "Why didn't you just say you expected him?"

"Just a minute," Noah cut in.

"Shut up," Alexander yelled. "I know your game. I know what you're after." He turned

118

back to Mickey, "What do you have to say for yourself?"

She was at first so filled with anger that she couldn't answer him, and then the same anger overflowed in cold, biting words. "I have nothing to say. And there's no reason I know of that requires I explain to you anything that I do."

"If you wanted to go out I would have taken you," he said furiously. "All you had to do was say what you wanted."

"I didn't want to go out with you," she retorted. "I hope that's plain enough, Alexander." She started for the door.

He caught her arm, fingers clutching, bruising.

Noah, lithe, quick, moving with tigerish grace, moved between Alexander and Mickey. A flashing hand fell on Alexander's pudgy shoulder, jerked him aside. "You're forgetting yourself, brother."

Alexander divided an enraged look between Mickey and Noah, and then stalked inside.

Noah grinned at Mickey. "There you have it," he said softly. "The two Warren boys losing their heads for love of you."

She didn't answer him.

She turned blindly away and stumbled indoors.

9

The next morning, although she delayed until later than usual hoping to avoid Alexander, Mickey found him waiting for her when she went downstairs.

She greeted him quickly, started past him.

He barred the way, his plump face flushed. "Mickey, I have to talk to you."

Runyon appeared in the doorway, gave them a quick curious glance, and said, "If you got a minute before you go, Alexander . . ."

"Later," Alexander told him.

He massaged his big jaw, rumpled his already rumpled pink hair, winked at Mickey, and disappeared into the living room.

Mickey said, "Let's forget it."

"I want you to understand. I want to apologize. I . . ."

He stopped because Winifred, wearing slate gray, came down the broad steps.

"Not gone yet?" she asked Alexander. "Shall I tell Bevis about your eggs?" And to Mickey, "The usual coffee?" She went on, stately as an ocean liner, taking for granted their assent.

"How can I talk here?" Alexander pleaded.

Mickey allowed him to draw her to the porch.

"You look haggard," Alexander said. "I hope . . . oh, Mickey, I hope you weren't upset at . . . at the way I acted last night. You do understand, don't you? I lost my head, I admit it. I made a fool of myself. I'm sorry."

"It doesn't matter," she told him, without much interest.

"But it does! Don't you see, Mickey? It's only because I love you. I want to take care of you, cherish you. I want . . ."

She stared at him, bewildered as well as angered.

Why didn't he realize that to say such a thing so soon after Bennett's death was an insult to Bennett and to her? Why didn't Alexander know that she had absolutely none of that feeling for him?

He hurried on, "It's always been like that between us. Don't you remember when we were kids?"

But she remembered only that he had teased her, played with her only when he could find nothing else to do. She remembered only that she had played with him when Noah wandered off . . .

And Alexander cried, "Then it's Noah."

Her cheeks burned with sudden heat.

"He is irresponsible," Alexander said

harshly. "Ruthless. You know that, Mickey."

She looked coldly into Alexander's plump face. "We can drop the subject now."

A startled flash shone briefly in his eyes, then faded.

She knew that her definite tone had gotten through to him.

But he said, "There is hope for me, isn't there? I can make you happy."

"I'm going inside." She suited action to the words, then turned back. "Alexander, remember my father's papers this evening, will you?"

In the dining room, Mickey found Winifred obviously dawdling over coffee, and anxious for breakfast conversation.

"It will be a lovely day," she began.

Mickey nodded.

"What a pity Theodora takes so much sleep. I thought the three of us might have a walk along the canal." Winifred paused to fill a Spode coffee cup, passed it to Mickey. "Perhaps you and I could go?" She paused again, sighed. "We used to have such lovely times."

"I don't think I'll take a walk today," Mickey said.

Winifred's grayish-brown eyes looked wistful. "Somehow, dear child, forgive me, I have such an odd feeling. As if . . . oh, how does one say it?" She waited, but Mickey didn't say anything. "There's a sense of . . . of uneasiness in you. I want so to help. And then, this bickering with Alexander . . ."

"That wasn't important, Aunt Winifred."

Winifred gave Mickey an arch look. "But, of course not . . . a small lover's spat."

"Lover's spat?" Mickey asked coldly, "aren't you rather presuming a great deal?"

Two spots of red suddenly appeared on Winifred's cheeks. She said stiffly, "If so, I beg your pardon. I hardly meant to. But it seemed to me, in this last month, that you, and Alexander . . ."

"Oh, please . . ." Mickey said, feeling the need to placate Winifred, "please understand. I don't want any emotional attachments now. You can see . . . after all, Bennett . . ."

Winifred looked mollified. "You're so young. It's terrible for you to be alone. And you and Alexander are related. It's not as if . . ."

Mickey, suddenly furious, put down her coffee cup. It made a loud click in its saucer.

Winifred looked pained. "The Spode, dear."

Mickey rose. "Forget it, Aunt Winifred."

"But, my dear child . . ."

"I mean it. I won't change my mind," Mickey said.

It was late afternoon. Cool gray twilight had settled over the house.

Mickey sat in the big chair before the dormer window, a book on her lap, but her eyes on the fading leaves of the oak trees.

The honeysuckle was gone, the wistaria, too, and soon, she thought the big old oaks would be bare as well.

The house was very still, as if holding its breath.

She felt as if she, too, were holding her breath.

She didn't look forward to seeing Alexander at dinner. She was certain that he would be too jocular, taking her suggestion that they both forget the night before more literally than she wanted him to. And Winifred would be watching her, grayish-brown eyes speculative, probably wondering what had happened to change Mickey from soft-voiced acquiescence to cold-voiced anger.

She wasn't herself certain of what had happened. But she wasn't sorry for it. That was one thing settled at least. Surely Alexander, and Winifred, too, would realize that Mickey did not want to be wooed. And now, if Runyon could help her, could tell her what to do, how to protect herself from the phone calls, from whatever might come next . . .

She repressed a shiver of terror. Runyon would know. He would help her. She had to believe that.

With Bennett gone, there was no one else.

Unaccountably she thought of Noah. Noah, tall, lithe, moving with a tiger's grace to thrust Alexander away from her. Noah, bottomless dark eyes full of bitter mockery, had said softly, "There you have it. The two Warren boys losing their heads for love of you."

Her cheeks burned as she remembered the sweetness of being in his arms.

She was relieved that her thoughts were interrupted by a tap at the door, and Theodora calling, "Mickey, you there?"

Mickey said, "I'm here. Come in."

Theodora opened the door, stood on the threshold, looking not at Mickey, but at the room. "Listen," she said finally, "why do you insist on staying up here alone all the time. What's here, Mickey?"

"I find it pleasant." Mickey wondered if Theodora had been sent by Winifred on a subtle peace mission.

"Come downstairs though. I have a friend I want you to meet. Vivian. You'll like her. We're having tea."

Still relieved at the interruption of her thoughts, Mickey followed Theodora to the drawing room.

The girl to whom Theodora introduced Mickey was about twenty-eight, tall, slim, as polished as a high-fashion model. Her hair was midnight black and elaborately disarranged. Her eyes were black and elaborately painted. Her lips were a self-confident, and disdainful muted pink.

Theodora, giggling, suddenly as awkward as a teenager, said, "Mickey, this is Vivian Starr."

"So you're Mickey Mayfield," Vivian cooed in a husky voice. "I've heard so much about you and about Bassett Place."

Mickey, uncomfortably aware of Vivian's appraising look, forced herself to smile. She stayed for just long enough to have a cup of tea and to chat briefly.

On her way upstairs, she met Winifred.

"Better now, dear?" Winifred asked, grayish-brown eyes searching Mickey's face.

Mickey forced another smile. Instead of answering the question, she said, "Theodora has a friend in. They're in the drawing room."

"A friend? Mickey, dear, you don't mind, do you?"

"Mind? Oh, Aunt Winifred, of course not."

Winifred obviously intended to say more, but Mickey went on, so Winifred, white head high, surged into the drawing room.

It was from there that Mickey heard Winifred say in tones of surprise, "Vivian Starr, what are you doing here?"

Mickey didn't hear Vivian's reply.

Back in the chair before the dormer window, book once more in her lap, Mickey tried to concentrate, but couldn't.

She had hoped that sometime during the day she would see Runyon, have an opportunity to speak to him. But he had been busy with chores around the grounds, and she supposed that when he had something to tell her he would make the time to find her.

The twilight had faded into blue evening.

Soon Alexander would be home, if he weren't already.

It was nearly time to dress for dinner.

But Mickey didn't move. She wondered if Vivian Starr had been invited to stay, and hoped not, but didn't really know why.

There was a scraping sound outside. The bright rungs of an aluminum ladder wavered before the window, and swung in to settle against the wall. Moments later, Runyon appeared there, pink head bent to smile at her through the glass.

Mickey waved at him, remembering that there had been some vague talk about the gutters needing to be looked at, and wishing that Runyon could manage to do such tasks by day.

She was about to get up, to go to him, to suggest that morning would be soon enough to see to the gutters. She had just risen, her face turned toward him, when suddenly, the aluminum ladder seemed to shift, and Runyon tipped forward, pink hair flying, mouth working in a scream. He tipped forward, hit the window, and disappeared. But in that moment, Mickey, unable to reach him in time, unable to save him, had seen the stark terror on his face.

The falling ladder sent clattering echoes into the house, but through them, Mickey heard the awful thud of body tumbling through empty air to concrete.

Screaming, she ran through the soft pink light of the hall, down the steps, and out into the September night.

Alexander was already there, bending over Runyon.

Theodora came trotting out just behind Mickey.

Winifred and Bevis struggled together in the doorway, until Bevis, out of habit, waited to allow Winifred to go first.

But it was Bevis who reached Runyon's side, and crouched there, emitting small unbelieving shrieks.

Time seemed to have stopped forever.

But then Alexander straightened up. He looked at Mickey. "I'm sorry," he said. "I'm sorry. Runyon's dead."

She knew that it must be true, yet her heart

made the denial. "No, Alexander. No. It's impossible."

She staggered back, feeling as if she, too, were being flung through space.

Bevis got to her feet. She gave Mickey a bitter look. "It's your fault," she said. "If you hadn't come back, then we wouldn't have been here. Then Runyon wouldn't be dead. It's your fault."

Quick hot tears blinded Mickey. Stumbling, she turned to escape Bevis' accusation. Arms came around her, held her in a moment of surprising sweetness. A voice said, "Bevis, that's quite enough."

Noah.

Noah holding her.

Noah whispering, "Mickey, it's a terrible accident. Don't look like that, Mickey."

She whispered, "It wasn't an accident. It couldn't have been."

Eyes stared at her — Alexander's blue, narrowed — Winifred's grayish-brown, cold — Bevis' blue, tear-drowned — Theodora's blue, wide.

Mickey turned within the circle of Noah's arms. She whispered against his shoulder once more. "It wasn't an accident," and knew she would never say it again.

They had told each other that the aluminum

ladder slipped on the concrete path. Poor Runyon fell and was killed. They buried him, and within a few days they forgot him.

But Bevis, working wildly, eyes red and pink hair in strings, remembered.

And Mickey remembered.

She had told Runyon of her terror, and he died.

Bennett was gone.

Runyon was gone. Who had told him the gutters must be cleaned?

She was alone. Alone and waiting.

If the notes she gave Runyon were found, she was never told of it, and she was always afraid to ask.

She waited. First days passed, then a week.

She waited, and one day Bevis came with an arm full of packages. "These just came for you, Mickey."

"For me? I didn't order anything."

"Must be presents then," Bevis said impassively. "Where do you want them?"

"On the bed, please."

When Bevis had gone, Mickey studied the labels. Yes, the packages were addressed to her. They were from a Georgetown shop, she saw.

She wondered uneasily who could have sent her a gift, hoping that Alexander hadn't chosen that way of begging her to forgive an incident she wanted only to forget. She wondered uneasily, if within the wrappings, she would find a note written in black bat tracks on a white sheet of paper.

But when she opened the packages, there was no note. No words from Alexander. Nothing.

Just a sleek, obviously expensive silk dress, pale green, her size. A set of pale green lingerie, lace-trimmed, and embroidered. A pale green sweater.

She stared at them, a pulse beating in her throat. She searched the boxes again, shook out the tissue paper, studied the labels.

Her hands shook. The absence of any comment was even more troubling than if there had been one.

Winifred paused in the open doorway. "Mickey, I wanted to say . . . please, dear child, it is terrible about Runyon, of course. But such things happen. You must not brood." She paused. "Why, Mickey, dear, what on earth?"

Mickey raised a white face, bewildered, frightened gray eyes.

Runyon, misshapen, dwarfed, no matter what he had been, was more than anything agile.

It could not have been an accident.

"What is it?" Winifred demanded. "Are the

things you bought the wrong size? No matter, dear. We'll take them back." She came in, stroked the silk of the dress, the lingerie. "Yes, lovely. And you'll be able to get . . ."

"But I didn't buy them," Mickey cried, and instantly wished the words unsaid.

"Didn't buy them," Winifred echoed. "But, my dear . . ." She paused. "But who did? A gift? Of course. Yes. That's what you mean."

"There's no card."

Winifred laughed. "The store undoubtedly forgot to put it in. You know what sales help is these days. We'll just call, find out."

"No," Mickey objected. "We'd better not."

"Why not?"

Mickey forced calmness into her voice. "Thank you, Aunt Winifred. I'll do it myself."

A few minutes later, she did call, but she knew exactly what information she would receive. She remembered what she had learned at the florist. When she reached the proper department she was told that Mrs. Marion Bassett Mayfield had been in the day before, opened a charge account, and the name being known at the store, had been allowed to have sent to her home the items described. Mrs. Marion Bassett Mayfield was dark-haired, about five foot three, weighed slightly more than a hundred pounds. It was suggested, if there were any questions, that she, the Mrs. Mayfield on the phone, come in immediately to verify her signature.

Mickey said she would.

Winifred, hovering nearby, demanded, "What did you find out?" though she had obviously understood from Mickey's end of the conversation, for without waiting for a reply, she went on, "Did they say you were there?"

"But I wasn't."

"When was it, dear?"

"Yesterday."

"Yesterday? Let me see. Oh, yes, Mickey. You were so restless. You went into Georgetown, didn't you?" Winifred's icy eyes narrowed. "And the shop is in Georgetown."

Mickey swallowed a protest, shook her head.

Winifred went on. "Perhaps you forgot? It isn't anything to worry about. Still, you might have . . . you have been so upset, dear."

Mickey gathered the packages, rewrapped them, then retreated to her big chair.

Winifred sighed and left.

As soon as she was alone, Mickey made up her face, brushed her hair. She took purse and gloves, and the three boxes, and went out to the porch to wait for the cab she had called.

Winifred followed her outside. "Do you always ask for the same driver? Ben Johnson?"

"I know him."

"You know him?" Winifred said thoughtfully. "But how peculiar."

"Not at all. He used to work for my father years ago."

"Is that so?" Winifred said doubtfully.

Mickey stifled her impatience, telling herself that Winifred meant nothing by the inquisition.

"But, my dear, surely when you ask for a specific driver, you do have to wait longer?"

"I like having someone I know. And I like him."

"I see," Winifred said.

The cab soon pulled up, to Mickey's relief. She got in, with Winifred still watching her.

Ben Johnson grinned, "I thought you'd given up on me, I haven't heard from you in so long."

"A lot's happened."

He pulled down the driveway and into the street, with Winifred still watching from the porch. "A lot's happened like what?" he asked.

She had made up her mind since Runyon's death that she would never tell anyone else. Bevis was right. It was Mickey's fault that Runyon was dead. Why, how, she wasn't sure. But she knew now that she must keep her own counsel. Yet Ben Johnson wasn't involved. Maybe he, as an outsider, could see sense where she was unable to see sense.

"Is it bad?" he asked, his voice as sweet as honey.

She told him about the note, the phone calls. She reminded him about the flowers.

He didn't look at her as if there were something wrong with her, he took her seriously. He frowned into the mirror. "It's funny. I don't think I like that. No. I don't."

"And now these packages. Clothes I didn't order."

She hadn't mentioned Runyon. Somehow she couldn't. If she did, she would have to say aloud the word she didn't dare say — murder. The word she hardly dared think in the privacy of her mind.

Ben asked, "You want to go to the store those clothes come from? You want to ask about it?"

She nodded.

"Sure it wasn't a mistake some way?"

She laughed softly. "Listen, are you going to be like my Aunt Winifred? She suggested that I bought this stuff, and sent it to myself."

"That your Aunt Winifred looking down her nose at me from the front porch?" He grinned. "If so, I'm not going to be like her."

In a little while Ben dropped her off in front

135

of the shop, said he'd wait.

She went in.

The sales person at first took Mickey to be the Mrs. Mayfield who had been in the day before. Then she apologized, saying, "No, of course, I see now. You're like her, but not exactly. I mean, she's taller, a bit heavier. It's just the same general impression. As if you were sisters, you know."

Sisters? Mickey thought. Or . . . twins? Not identical twins. But twins just the same.

The signature, nothing like Mickey's, was written in black ink.

Mickey closed the account, paid by check for the clothes.

Back in the cab she insisted Ben take them for his daughter Mallie.

He agreed unwillingly. "You ought to have left them in the store. But I can see how you wouldn't want them . . . But it means something, and I don't like it. Hadn't you better go to the police?"

"The police?" She shivered. "But I wouldn't know what to tell them. Nothing's really happened."

And she could imagine how Winifred, all the Warrens would look at her, if she did such a thing.

In spite of the sun, she was cold.

They drove through the gates, and she

looked through blurring tears at the gas-lights, remembering that Runyon had said as long as they burned all was well in Bassett Place.

As she went into the house, the phone rang.

Bevis came into the hall, saw her and retreated.

Mickey picked up the receiver, said, "Yes?" in a shaking voice.

There was the hum of the empty wire, the long slow breaths, and then, suddenly, faintly and far away, the sound of a giggle. A giggle, and a whisper, *"I know you. But you don't know me."*

Mickey gasped. "Who is this?"

The phone clicked in her ear.

She put down the receiver, retreated to her room, and listened to the whisper of sound that trickled thinly through the old house.

Later that evening, after cocktails in the drawing room where Winifred preferred that they be served as in the old days, after a slow and grueling dinner, while Theodora told Alexander, carefully not looking at Mickey, about the convertible she had been trying out, Mickey again retreated to her room.

Alexander had at last brought her the first set of her father's papers. He'd bent his pudgy body in a small ironic bow and said, "I hope you can understand these. If there are questions . . ."

She had thanked him hastily.

Now she settled at the desk, hoping, as he had, but without irony, that she would be able to figure out the details of her fortune. It seemed an impossible job. She studied lists of securities, bonds, investments. She looked at figures that had no meaning for her. Eventually, she came upon a package of letters tied in a cord.

When she opened them, she found that they pertained to her adoption. Her hands shook as she leafed through them. Her eyes burned with tears as she read her adoption papers.

They had made her the Bassetts' daughter, their child, and their heir.

She could have been anyone, anyone at all.

But she was not.

The Bassetts had chosen her, loved her.

She belonged with them when they were alive, and belonged to them still, now that they were dead.

She smoothed the papers carefully. There was a wrinkle, a twist, in the thick sheaf. She shook it, and a small, crumpled sheet fell out.

It was a brief note, handwritten on aging paper, and signed Boris Markham, M.D. It was dated October 23, 1943.

Mickey read, gray eyes widening, the words

that seemed to flicker and fade on the paper. "It appears now," the shifting words said, "that the young lady will be delivered of twins. In view of our arrangement, I feel you should be notified. Please communicate with me at once."

The young lady in question will be delivered of twins . . .

Twins.

10

The wind rustled sibilant words in the oak trees.

I know you. But you don't know me.

There had been two children born to that beautiful young girl whose soldier husband died in Italy. Two children.

One became Mickey Bassett.

And the other?

Where was the other now?

Had she been, like Mickey, lucky, and chosen and loved?

Or had she drifted, always alone, frightened, deprived?

Somewhere, Mickey thought, there was a part of herself waiting to be found, wanting to be found, hoping to be found.

I know you. But you don't know me.

The phone calls, long slow breaths, and at last, a faint and faraway giggle. The huge spray of twinberry. The clothes that would fit Mickey . . .

She put the papers away, the note from Dr. Markham, with the others, carefully replaced as she had found it.

Twins.

Winifred had known of the adoption. Had she also known that Mickey was one of twins? And knowing that, had she then developed her preoccupation with them?

In her excitement, Mickey couldn't wait. She felt very close to the explanation of everything that had happened since her return to Bassett Place.

She hurried downstairs. As she reached the living room, she heard Winifred's even voice.

". . . so strange. Really. Those pretty clothes. And she said she hadn't bought them. Denied it!"

"Wish she'd given them to me if she didn't like them," Theodora put in. "She didn't bring them home."

"Be quiet, Theodora." Winifred issued the peremptory order, and went on in the same breath. ". . . denied it to my face. And off she went with that colored taxi driver she always calls. Because she likes him, she said. And when she came back, well, I didn't dare ask her what it was all about. I thought that at dinner . . . but you saw her face . . . strange . . . And the way she reacted to Runyon's death . . . 'not an accident,' she said. Not an accident, indeed."

Shamed to listen, yet frozen, unable to move, Mickey heard it all, and imagined the looks the Warrens would be exchanging, eyes saying plainly that they believed what Winifred had almost, but not quite, put into words.

The familiar fear swept over Mickey.

But it was not the house whispering now. It was the Warrens. And it was her own doubt as well.

Had she stumbled into madness the moment she entered Bassett Place?

She took a deep, calming breath, and smoothed her dark curls. No. No, she was not being misled by a disordered mind. There were questions to be answered, and with the answers she would understand.

She called, "Aunt Winifred, I'd like to talk to you," and went into the living room.

Winifred and Alexander exchanged obviously embarrassed looks. Theodora laughed. And Noah sat in a lounge chair, frowning.

"Oh, I didn't know you were here, Noah," Mickey said.

"Came in a little while ago." Noah's bottomless dark eyes were noncommital.

A shiver went over Mickey. The Warrens had gathered for a conference. A conference about her.

"Sit down," Alexander told her. "Tell us what's wrong. You're as white as a sheet."

Noah, watching her, still frowned.

"Is it because of the papers, Mickey? I was afraid of that. It's always disturbing to . . ."

She turned to Winifred. "I found the adoption papers. And a letter from a Dr. Markham."

Alexander looked worried. "Are you all right? The way you look . . . perhaps we could have a doctor." He appealed to his mother. "Oughtn't we to call someone?"

Mickey ignored him. "Aunt Winifred, you knew that my real mother was to have twins, didn't you?"

"Twins?" Winifred echoed. Then, thoughtfully, "Well, I do believe I heard it mentioned once." She smiled her empty smile. "I don't know what happened. I suppose Benjamin wanted only one child."

"And what about the other one?" Mickey demanded.

"Why, dear, how would I know?"

"You don't have any idea?"

"Mickey, dear, it was never discussed. Do calm yourself. You are so distraught. It's unhealthy for you."

"Then where is my twin?"

Noah said softly, "It doesn't matter, Mickey."

"But it does," she cried.

"I'm sorry that I can not set your mind at rest," Winifred told her. "I know nothing about it."

"Nor do any of us, of course," Alexander said.

Theodora muttered sulkily, "And what difference does it make anyway?"

"I must find her," Mickey said.

Upstairs, pacing the room, she tried to think what to do.

She was certain that the calls, the note, the flowers, the clothes, were all connected in some way with her unknown twin. *I know you. But you don't know me.* Her twin had somehow located her, knew her . . . And now . . . now what? Mickey asked herself desperately.

Winifred, Alexander, Theodora, had all denied any knowledge of her twin. But Noah had been silent. Why had he been so silent, frowning as he watched her?

As she readied herself for bed, Mickey remembered how the Warrens had looked at each other, then looked at her.

She was all alone.

But somewhere, somewhere nearby, there was a girl who was part of herself, a girl enough like her to be mistaken for her by the saleswoman in the Georgetown shop, by the elderly florist. Mickey knew that she had to find her.

The house seemed to whisper around her as Mickey at last fell asleep.

"I don't like this neighborhood," Ben Johnson said doubtfully, shoving his red baseball cap to one side of his white curls.

She had told him about the doctor's letter, about her twin. Ben hadn't asked, "What difference does it make?" Instead, he asked, "What do you want to do?" and when she explained, he agreed, "Yep, that's an idea."

But now he grumbled, "No place for a doctor's office."

"He died, they told me. She sold their house, and moved in with her children. But later on, she came here, the old neighbors said. So it must be right."

He shook his head.

But she got out of the cab, crossed the sidewalk to the paint-blistered gate, and went up the leaf-littered path to the same, sagging clapboard house, from which blank windows glared empty and unwelcoming.

An old woman, bent and angry, answered her knock, demanded, "What do you want?"

Mickey introduced herself, asked if she could step in for a moment.

"I don't want to buy anything. Can't afford it."

"I'm not selling anything," Mickey said quickly.

The old woman's faded eyes moved from the small tan beret on Mickey's curls to the small tan shoes on her feet. "Guess you're not. Well, then?"

"You are Mrs. Markham? Your husband

was the doctor?"

"That's right enough. For all the good it did me." The old woman jerked the door open. "Come in. What do you want?"

The barrier of ungraciousness made it hard for Mickey to explain. She smiled diffidently. "It's complicated."

"Anything connected with Boris was complicated."

Mickey drew a deep breath. "My parents adopted me, in 1943 with Dr. Markham's help. I've learned that there was another child, my twin. I want to locate her."

"Ask your parents."

"They're both dead, Mrs. Markham."

"You're on a foolish errand. What's done is done. Don't fiddle with the past."

"But there must be records, something, to show what happened."

"Why do you want to know?"

"Because . . . because I am . . . I am alone, Mrs. Markham. But somewhere I have a sister. And . . . well, there were the two of us. I became the Bassetts' daughter. I was so lucky. I have so much. I want to . . . to share it all."

The old woman's face softened, but she shook her head. "You can't change what happened. And Boris' records are God knows where."

"And my name doesn't mean anything to you?"

"To me?" Mrs. Markham laughed bitterly. "Hardly. Why should it? You think I cared? Look around you. See what all his do-gooding got me." Her face softened again. "And you'd be smart to forget it."

Ben, when Mickey told him, agreed. "That's a sensible old lady. Crazy things happen in life. You can't change it. Do like she said. Forget it."

He repeated it with a worried look when he dropped her off at the house.

Winifred stopped her in the hall. "Dear child, what are you doing? We are all so concerned. We just . . . we just don't understand."

"It's all right," Mickey said.

"But, dear . . ."

Mickey took off her tan beret, ruffled her curls. "I'm going to find my twin."

Winifred sighed. "Really, dear." And then, "I hoped we might talk about having a small . . . well, a gathering perhaps. I introduce you around. I mentioned it once, remember, and this seems . . ."

"Not now," Mickey told her, and went upstairs.

The twins . . . dolls . . . dogs. Matching clothes on Noah and Alexander. The ruffled dresses bought for Theodora and Mickey, to which Mickey's mother had taken such exception. All that added up to Winifred's fascination with the idea of twins. And Winifred had known about Mickey's twin.

Mickey asked herself if having known Mickey was adopted, known that Mickey was one of a pair of twins, Winifred had planned, after telling her of the adoption, to then tell her about the twin.

What a terribly cruel thing to do to a child.

Mickey could remember her father saying that.

Had Winifred, frightened by Mickey's reaction, then decided not to tell Mickey the rest of it?

She winced, not wanting to think such thoughts.

Yet they were there in her mind and had to be faced.

The phone gave its discreet ring.

Heart beating wildly, she snatched it up. She hoped, prayed, that it would be the call she had been waiting for.

She cried, "Yes?" and heard the long slow breaths, and went on, "Don't hang up. Please, Please. I know who you are now."

There was an instant of silence. Then a distant giggle drifted over the wires.

"Please," Mickey begged. "Talk to me. Don't hang up."

And then there was a voice. "You know me?"

"Yes, yes, I do, and listen, I want to meet you."

"To meet me?" There was another silence. "But how do I know what you'll do?"

"We're sisters. I won't hurt you. I just want to meet you. Name a place, a time."

"Sisters." There was another pause. The wires hummed.

Mickey held her breath, waiting.

"But . . ."

"We . . . we have to get to know each other," Mickey cried. "Please . . . please don't hang up."

"I'll call you," the faint voice said.

"Tell me where to meet you."

Then, sulkily, "Oh, all right. Lincoln Memorial? Tomorrow? Ten o'clock?"

"Yes," Mickey agreed.

The phone clicked. The empty wire hummed.

Mickey replaced the receiver with trembling hands.

Tomorrow, she thought, at ten.

Noah had come by that evening, invited her to go for a ride. She was happy to escape the question in Alexander's blue eyes, the unconcealed concern in Winifred's, the indifference in Theodora's. But now, driving under the twinkling October stars, it was Noah who asked the questions.

"Mickey, what's happening to you?"

She sighed, but didn't answer.

"You seem so . . . so aloof . . . so . . . ."

"I have things on my mind, Noah."

He slanted a sideways look at her. "Mickey, this business about the twins . . . it's not wise."

She shrugged.

"What do you have in your mind? I want to know, Mickey. I have to know."

"I've found her," Mickey said softly. "I'm going to meet her tomorrow."

"Found her?" His voice was harsh with astonishment. "How could you?"

But she wasn't going to tell him how. She shrugged again.

"Listen," he said. "Leave it alone, Mickey."

She whispered, "No, no. I can't."

"Leave it alone," he repeated, and that time it seemed to her that his voice was harsh with menace.

But when they returned to the house, and she started to get out of the car, he slipped an arm around her shoulders. "Wait, Mickey."

She sat very still under his touch.

"I wanted to give you time," he said quietly.

"But since Alexander is pushing his suit . . ."
The skeptical twist was on his mouth. His deep dark eyes mocked her.

She said, "I think that particular joke has gone far enough."

"Joke? Poor Alexander wouldn't be happy to hear you call it that, Mickey."

"And you?" she heard herself ask, heard herself with horror.

"I?" The mockery was gone from his eyes. He said soberly, "You know how I feel about you."

"That was ridiculous of me," she whispered, "to lead you into saying that. I apologize, Noah."

"You apologize?" he said blankly.

She nodded, opened the door.

He followed her up to the porch. "Mickey . . . this business about the twin. You can't know who she is, what she is. At least explain it all to me. Let me check around for you . . ."

She looked up at him, shook her head.

He took her face between his hands. He bent his dark head to hers. His lips were warm, demanding, pressed to hers in a kiss that lasted only moments yet seemed endless.

Sweet, electrifying pulses throbbed through her. She was lost, lost. There was only Noah.

But then he let her go. He drew back.

He said lightly, "Now it's my turn to apologize."

"What do you mean?" she gasped.

"First things come first, Mickey. If you're going to trot off on silly trails after missing relatives, you can't have time to think of me."

She pulled away from him. "All this?" she asked coldly, "And just to dissuade me from doing what I am going to do?"

"Mickey . . ."

"I wonder why you think it so important."

He stared at her, fury in his dark eyes, his mouth hard. He jammed his hands in his pockets, and went back to the car.

By the time she had opened the door, the car was gone, fleeing past the flickering gaslights at the gate.

Still trembling, she went inside, rubbing the sweet kiss, the false kiss, from her lips.

11

It was ten o'clock. A pale sun shone on white marble, cast thin shadows along the long, austere flights of steps.

Mickey waited, eyes strained, heart thudding, shivering within her heavy tweed suit.

Half an hour earlier, Winifred, plainly not wanting to ask directly, but hinting to know where Mickey was going, had said, "Rather a nasty day, dear. Perhaps you ought to stay at home."

"I won't be long," Mickey had told her, aware of the watching eyes that followed her into the cab.

And Ben, giving her a worried look as he maneuvered the driveway, asked, "Are you sure you want to do this?"

But she had to meet the girl with the whispery voice. She had to meet her sister, her twin.

Why were the Warrens so insistent that it was wrong of her to look for her only real relative?

Did they believe Mickey was being deceived in some way?

Did they think her mad?

Or . . . Mickey winced . . . were they thinking about the Bassett fortune? Winifred and
Theodora both often spoke wistfully of
money. Alexander was ambitious. And Noah
. . .

She wouldn't let herself think of Noah.

She glanced at her wrist watch. It was just
moments after ten. She studied the steps nervously, waiting, buoyed by hope.

The big statue behind her, seated on a marble throne, seemed to watch her with com-
passionate gaze and set somber lips.

A guard glanced at her, then went on.

A small boy, tugging at his father's leg, demanded, "Who's Lincoln, Daddy?"

Mickey studied the steps, and studied her
watch, and waited.

At noon, she gave up.

Ben, parked where she had left him, looked
relieved when she appeared.

She got into the cab wearily.

"No go, hunh?" he asked.

She shook her head.

"Better. Yep. I think it's better."

"She ought to have come."

"And I think you should tell the police. It's
some kind of con game." Ben's voice was gentle. "You don't want it to be, but that's what
it is."

"I have to find her," Mickey answered, in

a voice near tears.

He sighed. "She'll call again."

And he was right.

That same afternoon, Mickey's hopes were rewarded. The phone gave its signalling ring. The whispery voice asked, "Mickey, is that you?"

"Why weren't you there?" Mickey cried.

"I couldn't come."

"Then when? Where?"

"It's more complicated than you think, Mickey."

"Just meet me. We'll talk about it then."

"Tomorrow. The Botanical Gardens. Twelve o'clock."

"I'll be there," Mickey promised.

"And so will I," the whispery voice told her.

That night at dinner, Alexander asked jocularly, "And what did you do today, Mickey?"

She didn't answer.

But Winifred said, "Mickey went out. She stayed out for hours. And when she came home . . ."

"Did something happen, dear?" Alexander asked.

"Nothing," Mickey retorted.

Winifred sounded as if she were about to weep, although her expressionless face was as blank as always, "It must be something. She looked about to faint when she came home. What are we going to do, Alexander?"

Mickey cried, "You can stop acting as if I'm subnormal . . . or as if I am mad!"

The candlelight seemed to flicker, throwing huge black shadows on the walls.

Winifred gasped, "Mickey, what an odd thing to say!"

Alexander leaned forward, smiling. "Mickey, surely you understand that we're worried about you. What you need is to go out, enjoy yourself, give up this childish obsession. There's a good topical comic at the Shoreham. Suppose we go there tonight?"

"No, Alexander, not tonight," Mickey said. "But thank you."

"But how can we help?" Winifred asked, looking at Alexander.

"Ask Noah," Alexander retorted.

Mickey said nothing at all.

The air was hot, steamy, sweet with the overpowering scent of tropical plants. The glass roof refracted the pale October sun, making a glare that burned Mickey's eyes.

She peered past fern and leaf and vine at the big door.

She listened through humming machinery and rustling foliage for the sound of footsteps.

She waited from noon until two o'clock.

At last, Ben came in search of her. "No use standing here any more."

"She didn't come," Mickey said blankly.

He led her to the cab, drove her back to the house.

She paid him, thanked him.

"Forget it," he begged.

But she shook her head. "Maybe she'll call again."

But it was two days, two long, dragging, empty days, before the whispery voice returned, said, "I couldn't make it. I'm sorry, Mickey."

"I don't understand," Mickey cried. "Why do you do it? I promise I won't hurt you. Why can't we meet?"

"I'll be there," the whispery voice giggled. "Honest, this time I will. I told you it was more complicated than you thought."

"I'll wait for you at Fletcher's Landing. Just off Canal Road. Tomorrow, at five."

"All right." It was grudging agreement, but it was agreement. "Tomorrow. At five."

"Don't you want to tell me about it?" Noah asked.

"About what?" Mickey rolled an unlit cigarette between her fingers.

He said sharply, "Don't be ridiculous."

"Really, Noah."

"Really, Noah," he mocked her. "You've

got Winifred and Alexander almost in a panic, trying to figure you out."

"There's nothing to figure out."

"You said you'd found your twin. And now . . ."

"I'm going to meet her. Tomorrow."

"You've said that before."

"There was a delay."

"I see . . . How did you manage to find her, Mickey?"

But she didn't trust him. She didn't dare to.

"It's a long story."

"I have lots of time."

She demanded, "Did Winifred and Alexander tell you to cross-examine me this way?"

"I run nobody's errands but my own," he snapped. "I ask nobody's questions but my own." He rose, hands jammed in his pockets. "I'm afraid you're lighting matches in a haystack."

She thought that she might be. It didn't matter. It was her haystack, her matches. Since Runyon had died, there was no one involved but herself.

She said finally, "What I do is my business, Noah."

His face softened. He smiled. "Of course. You're all grown up now, aren't you? Forgive my concern."

It was hard to believe, then, looking into his dark eyes, that he might be wearing a mask that concealed the signs that he was against her.

But when she was alone, she asked herself if his questions were based on concern for her, or if they were based on concern for some plan of which only he was aware.

She asked herself why Winifred, and Alexander, and Theodora, kept insisting that there was something wrong with her.

There was nothing wrong. The time of the long and living shadow was far behind her.

It was not irrational to want to find all that was left in the world of her flesh and blood.

Noah and Alexander . . . both pretending to court her.

Theodora hinting about the convertible.

Winifred . . .

And there was the Bassett fortune.

Mickey thrust the ugly thought away.

"I'm not going to leave you," Ben said, his mouth set stubbornly. "I don't like it. It scares me."

"But if you stay, she might not come. And I just couldn't bear being disappointed again."

"Then get set for it. But you wait and see. One of these times, she will come. She wants something."

"I'm the one that wants something."

"Maybe." But his reply was only courtesy.

He eased the cab to a stop. "Remember where you go? You haven't been here for a long time."

She nodded.

"I'll be close. And don't wait too long."

She promised him, and herself, that she wouldn't. But at six, with dusk settling, with the cold night wind beginning to stir the trees, now almost bare, she was still waiting.

She paced the soggy ground near the boathouse, her eyes fixed on the path that led down from the canal.

A mockingbird trilled off to her left, and she turned to look for it, and a sound somewhere along the path made her swing back, her heart jumping with hope.

But it was Ben. "It's over an hour. That's long enough."

She wanted to stay a little longer, but she knew he was right. She followed him back to the cab.

It was one more failure.

"What will I do if she doesn't ever call me again?"

"Forget it."

"Oh, why didn't I get her name, find out where she lives? Why . . ."

"She'll call again."

Mickey waited, keyed up, tense. Her eyes grew larger in her small face. Her wrists grew more fragile. She couldn't sit still, but prowled the house, listening for the old whispers.

Winifred suggested shopping trips, suggested a gathering. Alexander was jocular, and baffled. Theodora stayed out of her way. Noah came to see her, gave her a mocking grin and said, "And you informed me you were all grown up, Mickey."

She was grown up, she thought then. She was struggling alone to do what she must do, to resolve doubt with certainty, as Bennett had told her.

She waited through a haze of numb hope, and fought the familiar fear with all her strength. She knew that her twin was real. She had not come home to return to the valley of the long and living shadow . . .

On the third day, as Mickey passed through the hall, the phone rang. She answered and cried, "Yes? Hello?"

"It's me," the whispery voice said. "I couldn't help standing you up. But now . . . if you still want me to, I've decided, and I'll be there."

"Then come to my house," Mickey said.

"To your house! Oh, no! The deal's off if you . . ." The frightened whisper paused.

Mickey said quickly, "All right. Where? But

don't be afraid of me. Please. Please."

"Tomorrow then. Noon. Woodward and Lothrop's. The scarf department on the first floor."

"Yes. But please . . . this time be there."

"You be there, too."

Mickey was fervent. "Oh, I will."

12

The scarves were silken, and streamed across the counter like shining rainbows.

Droves of women fluttered around them like hovering birds.

Mickey, looking beyond them, saw Ben's reassuring nod.

He had insisted on parking the cab in the garage, on coming inside with her.

She, thinking ahead too hard to argue with him, had agreed.

Now she waited, scanning the faces of the women who brushed by, certain that when she saw her twin she would instantly recognize her.

It was two minutes past noon.

A shrill voice said, "Mickey Mayfield?"

"You did come!" Mickey cried, and stared, wordless then, at the girl who grinned at her.

This was her sister, her twin.

She had expected to feel something.

She ought to feel something.

Yet they were strangers. It was unbelievable that they could be flesh and blood and still be strangers.

The girl said uneasily, "I guess you're disappointed, aren't you?"

She was slightly taller than Mickey, slightly heavier. She wore a garish imitation leather suit in shiny red. Her spike-heeled shoes were patent leather. Long earrings dangled from under an elaborate hairdo of short black curls.

Mickey smiled. "I'm so glad to meet you finally. I can see . . . see the resemblance, can't you?"

"Sure. It's there all right . . . And I'm sorry about those other times."

"Let's go some place where we can talk." Mickey laughed then. "Why, I don't even know your name!"

I know you. But you don't know me.

The words flashed through Mickey's mind.

"I'm Martha. Martha Plainard." She grinned. "Mickey and Marty. Sort of go together, don't they?"

Marty had a shrill voice, with something of a Southern slur in her words.

Mickey felt ashamed to have noticed that Marty didn't sound like a Washingtonian, ashamed to have noticed Marty's garish outfit.

She took Marty's arm, nodded at Ben, and led Marty up the escalator to the seventh floor tea room.

There, with sodas ordered, for Marty had wrinkled her nose at the suggestion of tea, Mickey wondered how to begin.

Marty shifted uneasily. "I've never been here before."

Mickey ignored that, leaned forward. "Now, tell me . . ."

A look of fright passed over Marty's face. "Tell you what? And anyway, what do you want? Why did you want to meet me?"

"We're sisters. We're twins. How did you know, Marty? How did you find out . . . And why . . ."

"You sure are full of questions, Mickey."

"I want to catch up. And I want to understand."

"You mean you want to make sure I'm not some kind of a phony, don't you?"

Mickey protested.

But Martha laughed. "Oh, come on. Admit it! And I don't blame you. For all you know I could be a con artist. O.K. I'll tell you how it was. You got picked by the Bassetts, so you were on easy street. I got left. I bounced from one foster home to another. Nobody wanted me except for the payments they got from the government. So then . . ."

"But your mother's name? Your father's?"

Marty laughed. "Wise guy, aren't you?" She went on, "I never knew that any more than you did. And when I was about fifteen, I got interested, see? Just like you got interested, I guess. Only you took a lot longer. So I

165

checked back through the foster homes. All I came up with was the name of a doctor. Markham. I went to see him. He said he didn't know a thing. But when I left, I listened outside the door." She gave Mickey a defiant look. "I heard him mumbling something about the Bassetts. I went back in, figuring that was my folks' real name. I threw it in his face. He got upset. He finally told me my mother's and father's name, and what happened to them. I asked what any Bassetts had to do with it, so he said I was mixed up, they didn't have anything to do with it."

"Then how did you find out . . ."

"From the papers," Marty giggled, a familiar sound but close this time. "A couple of years later, I saw your picture. You were going away to school. Soon as I saw it I figured we were sisters, twins. That's what the doc wouldn't tell me. So from then on, I was real interested in you. And I followed your doings pretty good. Being the Bassett girl," she added bitterly, "You got mentioned. People paid attention to you."

"And just from thinking that we look a little bit alike . . ."

Marty grinned. "Oh, no. I went and saw your mother. Your adopted mother. I asked her straight out. She said I was all wet, but she was scared. So I was sure I was right.

But you got married, and moved away. When your folks died and you came back, there was a picture, too. The same one as they had from your wedding, I guess, and the article, too, saying about you." Marty shrugged. "I figured . . . oh, I don't know exactly, but I wanted you to know about me. I thought it wasn't fair. Not that I expected anything," she added hastily. "I mean . . . why should you care about me? But still . . . anyhow, I wrote the note. I called you a couple of times. I even sent you those honeysuckle sprays, cost me plenty, and there were the clothes . . ."

"But Marty, why didn't you sign your name, get in touch with me?"

"Well, I wanted to in a way. But I guess . . ." Marty grinned, ". . . maybe I was afraid you'd say 'Who are you?' and kick me out or something." She paused, then went on. "I'm sorry about getting you stirred up. I am. Real sorry. And I'm sorry about not showing up those other times, when I said I would." A momentary look of fright touched her face. "There's a lot you don't understand, see?"

"But you are my sister, Marty. We have to get to know each other."

"Sure. But it's different for you. You can do what you want. You don't have to look after yourself."

"Where do you work?"

"I'm not working right now."

"Then how do you live?"

"Oh, I manage. Don't worry about me."

Mickey found herself tearing her paper napkin into tiny shreds. There was one question she wanted to put to Marty, but didn't know how to phrase it.

Then Marty, with a twist of bitterness on her very pink lips, said, "But I guess, you being a Bassett, you don't worry about much."

It was the twist of bitterness that told Mickey why, having been interested in her, followed her, all those years, Marty had suddenly begun to call, to leave the notes that said "I know you, but you don't know me," to send the flowers and charge the clothes. Poor Marty, jealous, wanting the kind of life that Mickey took for granted, had tried to force her way into Mickey's life, but had probably been too afraid to come forward honestly and openly.

Afraid.

Mickey understood that, and in understanding, found it easy to forgive Marty.

The napkin shreds drifted like snow flakes across the table top as Marty suddenly thrust back her chair.

"Wait," Mickey cried, her mind made up, knowing, without thinking about it, what she wanted to do.

Marty gave her a wry grin. "O.K. You've met me. What else is there?"

"Come and live with me. We're sisters. We ought to be together. And . . . and I've wanted somebody . . . somebody to belong to for so long."

But Marty looked frightened. "Say, I couldn't do that! You sure do get carried away, don't you?"

"Why not?" Mickey grinned. "It's what you've always wanted, too, isn't it? It's why you . . . you contacted me. You know it is, Marty."

"Well . . . maybe . . ." A quick calculating look narrowed Marty's eyes. "But I'd have to think about it." Her face hardened. "And you better think about it, too."

"I know it's the right thing."

"Only I don't." Marty grinned. "Imagine! Me, nobody saying 'I have to think about it,' to you, a Bassett. As if I wouldn't jump at the chance."

"Then there's nothing to think about."

"Plenty." Marty went on slowly, her slightly slurred words a whisper. "And if you're smart, you won't say anything just yet. Not to the rest of them."

"Do you mean the Warrens?"

"That's who I mean. I'll bet they won't be happy to see me coming."

"But, Marty, how do you know about them?"

"Same way I knew about you. The papers, all that. And believe me, they'll have plenty to say about you bringing a stranger into the house."

"It's my house. And you're not a stranger."

"But wait until we really decide. O.K.?"

"If that's what you want."

Marty pushed back her chair again. "Then . . ."

"But wait a minute," Mickey cried. "I don't know where you live. Don't disappear again, Marty."

"I'll be in touch. Honest. In a couple of days," Marty promised.

They took the escalator down together. Mickey offered to have Ben drive Marty wherever she wanted to go, but Marty said no to that. With a grin and a wave, she faded into the crowd of women shoppers.

Mickey, watching, suddenly wondered if she would ever see Marty again.

Ben said, "You caught up with her finally."

By the time she was in the cab, heading back to Bassett Place, Mickey had convinced herself that Marty wasn't gone forever.

Ben asked, "What did she want with all her foolish tricks?"

"To know me," Mickey told him, and then

suddenly, knowing the reality, she was warm with joy. "Ben, I'm so happy. It was worth it all. Just finding her. And I want her to come and live with me . . . I want . . ."

He frowned, his worried eyes studying her in the rear view mirror. "Listen, it don't sound right to me. How much do you know about her? She ought to be checked out. I mean by somebody that knows how. Like a private detective. Yep, I mean it. You're a rich woman. There's plenty of folks wouldn't mind having some of your money."

She thought instantly of the Warrens.

Marty was right. They would let loose a flood of objections exactly like Ben's.

Mickey told him defensively, "She knew everything. Nobody else could have known."

"That's what you've got to find out."

But Mickey, wanting desperately to be sure of Marty, was sure of her, and once again began waiting hopefully for a call.

As they drove under the flickering gaslights at the gates of Bassett Place, she thought of Runyon, wishing that she could tell him her good news, sad that he would never know.

Those days after his death, when she had been so convinced that he couldn't have accidentally fallen from the ladder, seemed far away and unreal.

All that was real was the present.

Smiling to herself, Mickey began to make plans.

Two days later, Marty called. She sounded frightened, but determined, saying, "If you still mean it, then O.K. Sure, I'll move in with you."

Mickey laughed. "That's what I've been waiting to hear." She went on eagerly, "When?"

"Whenever you say."

"Tonight then. I'll have Ben pick you up."

"I'll get there myself, and with my stuff. Which isn't much." Marty giggled. "This is going to be fun."

"Eight? Nine?"

"Around then." Marty gave her faint giggle again. "See you."

The familiar faint giggle . . .

For a moment, Mickey shuddered, remembering.

But that was over now, she reminded herself, and warm with joy, she decided to tell the Warrens. It wouldn't be fair to Marty, or to them either, to give them no warning.

Mickey waited until they were having after-dinner coffee in the drawing room.

Noah, who had joined them unexpectedly, grinned at her. "You look like the cat that swallowed the canary."

She smiled. "I have something wonderful to tell you."

"Oh, a surprise." Winifred reared back, her piled-high white hair gleaming. She glanced at her watch. "But I do have bridge tonight. So that . . ." She paused. Then, "Alexander? Noah? Will either of you be here tonight? So that Mickey won't have to be . . ."

Theodora cut in petulantly. "I have a date tonight, Mother."

"I know that, dear. Which is why I didn't ask you."

Mickey said gently, "You won't have to worry about that any more. I've found my sister, my twin. She's coming to live with us. She's coming tonight."

The room was full of a dead silence. It hung like a weighty cloud, static, enveloping, smothering.

Alexander, his face flushed, shouted, "That's impossible! Impossible! What do you mean you found her?"

"I saw her today," Mickey said quietly.

"You saw her!" Alexander was on his feet, thick shoulders hunched. His suave pompous manner was gone. He seemed oddly threatening.

Noah, curt, hard-voiced, said, "Alexander!" Then asked Mickey, suddenly gentle, "How did you find her?"

The room seemed to be shrinking around her.

The waiting silence was filled with whispers.

The Warrens stared at her in disapproving disbelief.

She said finally, "In my father's papers there was that letter about the twin. I told you about it, remember?"

"Yes. But then . . . ?" Noah's bottomless dark eyes never left her face.

She bent her head. She couldn't tell them about the notes, the phone calls. If she really did explain, they would say that Marty should be investigated. They would find some way to send Marty away.

Mickey said finally, "That's a long story." She turned to Winifred. "You said you had a bridge game."

Winifred sat as if frozen. "Who is this girl? Where does she belong?"

"Her name is Martha Plainard. Everybody calls her Marty."

Alexander, his face mottled, leaned forward. "Mickey, as your lawyer, entrusted by Bennett to look after you, I must forbid this ridiculous step. You must give us time to make sure . . . to . . ."

"Leave her alone," Noah cut in, then went on to Mickey, "You should do exactly what you want, of course. But don't you think that you are being a little impulsive?"

But Mickey answered, "I hope you'll be good to Marty. She belongs with me."

Winifred heaved up from the plush sofa, put her Spode cup on the silver tray. "If your mind is made up, dear child, what can we do but pray for the best?" With that, she surged out of the room, murmuring, "Bridge, you know."

Theodora chuckled. "I never saw Mother give in so quickly. I'll have to take lessons from you, Mickey."

Alexander mumbled, "I'm going to the office," and went out, with Theodora following him.

Noah, grinning at Mickey, said, "You look quite smug with your bombshell, and the canary is certainly all gone."

"I'm very excited."

"I guess the objections weren't particularly cheering."

"I expected them, Noah."

"Shall I wait, welcome the new addition with you?"

She wondered why he was so anxious to see Marty that he couldn't delay until another time.

"No, thanks," she told him. "I'd rather you didn't."

Noah's dark brows rose. "Of course. Good

night then." He left her without another word.

It hadn't been easy, she thought, when she was alone. But it had been easier than she expected it to be. The Warrens had a right to be surprised, even to be suspicious. But they would get over that. They would have to.

It was a little after eight when she heard the car.

She jumped to her feet, rushed out to the porch, shivering as the cold air enwrapped her. The lights drifted down the road, stopped.

Mickey wondered why whoever had brought Marty didn't drive her directly up to the house.

She went down the steps, and into the driveway.

It was dark, shadowed.

Fading shrubbery obscured the road.

But she saw the car lights drift away, turn and come back. She saw the lights begin to move quickly.

Too quickly, she thought, and began to run.

But the thud was sudden and sharp and horrible.

And she knew what it was.

She knew what had happened.

She reached the gate as two winking red taillights disappeared around the far corner.

A smashed-open suitcase, its contents strewn about, lay in the middle of the street. Martha lay crumpled against the iron fence under the flickering gaslights.

13

"What's Mrs. Warren going to say?" Bevis asked. "You didn't eat anything."

"I'm not hungry." Mickey's voice was listless. She turned from the tray to look at the big dormer windows.

A gray mist hung on the bare limbs of the big oaks.

A gray sky hung over the river.

Bevis shrugged, and ran her hands through her pink hair, "Now it's two."

"Two?"

"Two deaths. Two accidents."

"And both my fault," Mickey whispered.

"Runyon always said such things came by threes."

Mickey shivered, continued to look at the window.

The door closed softly.

Bevis was gone.

Marty had lain crumpled against the iron fence, wide straining eyes filled with accusation.

Red taillights winked around a corner and were gone.

Mickey could remember screaming, a raw

awful sound that brought Bevis from the house.

The blinking red spots on police cars.

The ambulance siren shrilling closer and closer.

The questions, the answers.

Later, blinded by tears, she was led inside.

Winifred and Alexander, called by Bevis, arrived soon after.

They were shocked, but competent. They handled everything. Everything except the identification. Mickey had to do that.

A few hours later, a stolen car, front end damaged, with a bit of Marty's red skirt caught in its grill, was found on a side street off MacArthur Boulevard.

It was, the police said, a hit and run accident.

Mickey hysterically insisted that Marty had been killed by the same car that had brought her to the house, hysterically insisted that Marty had been murdered.

Alexander said, "It was the same thing with Runyon," and called a doctor.

He, with Winifred, spoke to the doctor just outside of Mickey's door.

She, listening, wondering if they meant for her to hear them.

Winifred said, "My niece had a breakdown once, Doctor. It was years ago. Of course, she's been . . . well, I should imagine one might say she's been a little . . . shaky since. Still, she did manage. But now . . . this . . . we're terribly afraid . . ."

"Because of her sister's death?" the unfamiliar voice asked.

"If it was her sister. We'll never know now. The police traced the poor girl. She had a room in town. She wasn't working, had no friends. It's hard to understand. But Mickey blames herself. And of course, if she hadn't gotten this ridiculous idea . . ."

Alexander put in, "And there was Runyon, too."

"Another accident," Winifred explained.

"I see," the unfamiliar voice rumbled.

Mickey, listening, trembled.

She had stumbled back into the valley of the long and living shadow.

The whispering in the house grew louder. The eyes stared.

She buried her head in the pillow and wept.

The doctor introduced himself, a firm hand on her shoulder. "I'm Dr. Baines, Mrs. Mayfield. I want to talk to you."

He was small, dapper. He had dead eyes. When she wouldn't talk to him, he gave her sedatives and departed.

In the week since, he had been back several times.

She was calm. She could speak to him. She could tell him that Marty had been murdered. But he talked of overstrained nerves, and overtired muscles.

He had no cure for what ailed her.

Now she sighed and sat up.

She was tired, worn out, wept out.

The days since Marty's death had passed in an odd disjointed dream, something between waking and sleeping.

It was time for her to get up.

Time . . . the only permanent anodyne for pain, Bennett had once told her.

She was alone again. Her parents gone, Runyon gone, Bennett gone, now Marty gone.

Everyone she had ever loved . . .

She struggled to her feet. She showered, put on a robe. She brushed her hair, avoiding a straight look into her gray eyes, into the thin white face that looked back at her. She used makeup to cover the haggard shadows. She was all dressed, exhausted, but still dressed, when Bevis came in.

"You're not supposed to be up yet," Bevis told her.

"Why not?"

Bevis backed out of the room.

Mickey heard the quick footsteps on the stairs.

Moments later, Winifred arrived, panting.

"Dear child, what are you doing?"

Mickey smoothed the blue wool dress on her narrow hips. "I've had too much rest."

"Don't you realize? Can't you see it for yourself? You've been very ill, dear child."

"I'm better now."

"But Dr. Baines . . ."

"Never mind, Aunt Winifred. I don't need any more sedatives."

Winifred sank heavily to the bed. "You are being so . . . so strange. I just don't know what to say. And after your terrible illness . . ."

"I was fourteen then, Aunt Winifred," Mickey said sharply.

"Yes, yes. But don't you know that you must be careful? And now . . . after what's happened . . . although you must admit, dear, we did try to warn you . . ."

"That's done, Aunt Winifred."

Winifred drew a long breath. "I'm sure you don't remember that night very well. But when Bevis called me away from my bridge game, and Alexander stopped by from the office, and we came here, you were . . . you raved and screamed and ran through the grounds." Winifred sighed. "It was . . . I am sorry to have to say this, but it was the same as the first time, Mickey. Exactly the same."

"Do you think so? I suppose I was terribly

upset. I'm sorry if I've frightened you. But I'm back to normal now."

Winifred heaved herself up. "You know best," she said doubtfully. "But your condition is worse than . . ." She let the words trail off. She smiled her empty smile, and went out of the room.

Alone, Mickey collapsed into the big chair near the dormer windows. She shook, and tears welled in her eyes, her body melting in familiar fear.

The only antidote for fear is courage, she told herself, using Bennett's words.

She fought for control and found it.

She had to know the truth. She had to know why Marty had been murdered.

She took a blue coat, her purse, and went downstairs. With the phone in her hand, she felt stronger, more clear-minded. She dialed quickly.

A plump, well-tended hand settled firmly on her fingers.

"What on earth are you doing?" Winifred asked reproachfully, and hastened on, "You can not go out yet. Please don't be a thoughtless, hysterical child."

"I thought I would take a ride, that's all, Aunt Winifred."

"It's too soon, dear. We'll have Bevis serve us tea. And perhaps we can have a game of cards. Before you know it, Alexander will be home."

Mickey agreed unwillingly.

Winifred surged ahead to the drawing room. "Come along, dear. Now where is that Bevis?"

"I wish you would put one on," Alexander said, bending over her. "A single rose pinned in your curls, Mickey."

She hid her face in the bouquet he had brought her. "Thank you, Alexander."

"But will you? For me?"

"Will I what?" she asked absently, and looking up at him.

She saw the worried glance he gave Winifred before he said gently, "Mickey, dear, weren't you paying any attention? I asked if you'd wear a rose in your hair. For me."

She shook her head, thrust the bouquet at him. "Would you ask Bevis to put these in water, please?"

He shot another worried look at Winifred, but said smoothly, pompously, "Of course I will." He started from the room, turned back to say, "You can't imagine how wonderful it is to have you downstairs again."

"Thank you, Alexander."

She rolled an unlit cigarette through her curled fist. It had been days, she wasn't sure how many, since she had seen Noah. She wondered why.

Theodora, crying, "Look who I ran into," and trailed by Vivian Starr, stopped in the doorway.

"How nice," Winifred said, giving Vivian an empty smile.

As sleek and well turned-out as always, Vivian grinned, seated herself in an easy chair as if it were a throne and she a queen.

Mickey barely listened while the three other women talked together. But she looked up at a moment's silence, caught Vivian staring at her, staring at her with an odd expression of anger.

"This is a surprise," Alexander said heartily, returning to the room just then.

"I was just leaving," Vivian told him.

"Oh?"

Mickey wondered why that single syllable sounded somehow approving.

"I'll see you to the door," Alexander went on.

Vivian said good-bye, then she and Alexander went out.

"We'll have dinner in a few minutes," Winifred said happily. "Are you ready for cocktails now?"

In the morning, a sodden wind tore the last

of the oak leaves away, leaving bare oak limbs silhouetted black against the gray sky. The river below the palisades ran dark and swift.

Mickey in raincoat and hat waited on the porch.

It was quite early.

She had come down quietly, slipped outside without seeing anyone. She wished that Ben would hurry.

Suddenly the door opened. Bevis cried, "Oh, it's you out here."

"I'm going for a little ride," Mickey told her.

"But you're not supposed to."

Mickey didn't answer her, and after hesitating for a moment, Bevis went indoors.

Mickey ran down the steps as Ben pulled into the driveway. As soon as he could, the cab barely stopped, he called, "How are you?"

She got in at once. "Let's go, Ben. Let's hurry."

He nodded, spun the cab down the driveway, and out into the street. Finally he asked, "Are you running away?"

"I guess I am. In a way . . . Ben, you know what happened, don't you?"

"Yep. I read about it in the paper. It's a shame. I called a couple of times. I was wondering about you."

"You called me, Ben? I didn't know that."

Her voice was small, frightened. "I don't know what to do. What to think."

"Accidents happen."

"Two accidents? First Runyon, then Marty." She swallowed hard. "Who next, Ben? They say such things run in threes."

"No," he protested.

"Marty's address, where she lived when she was coming to me, was in the papers." Mickey gave him the street and house number. "That's where I want to go."

"But why?"

"I want to know more about her, Ben. I don't think Runyon's death was an accident, and I don't think Marty's was either. I have to know if . . . if it's my fault, or if it was something else, something that had nothing to do with me."

14

Ben, still arguing that Mickey ought to forget Marty Plainard and what had happened, drove Mickey to the address she had given him.

They passed through Southwest, a section of the city, one of the older ones, that she hadn't seen in years.

There were blocks of desolation, areas bulldozed down. Then there were blocks of giant white concrete high-rise apartments set in narrow strips of parking lots and narrower strips of fading green. At last, lost once, found once, Ben turned into an old street, parked before an old house.

"I'd hardly believe this was still standing," he grumbled.

"Maybe it won't be for long."

Mickey went up to the weather-beaten brownstone house. There was a to-let sign in the window. The woman who answered Mickey's knock seemed disappointed to learn that Mickey wanted to ask about Martha Plainard, not about a room.

"Martha?" she sighed. "Sure she lived here. Until she got killed by that car. What about it?"

"Do you know where she came from? About her family?"

"No. She was just here three months. Had a couple of boy friends. Had an eye for a good thing maybe. She told me one time she was going to get her hands on . . ." The woman paused. "Who did you say you are? You look a lot like her."

"I'm a friend of hers."

"Then you ought to know more than me."

Mickey realized that the woman wouldn't tell her what she knew, if she knew anything. Mickey thanked her, returned to the cab.

"No luck?" Ben asked, as she got in.

"I guess it was a silly idea." She sighed. "But where else was there to try?"

"Ought to stop trying. You sound wore out. I'm going to take you home."

"I guess you'd better." She stopped, leaned forward. "Ben, listen, do you think . . . is it possible to deliberately drive somebody crazy?"

Ben chuckled, "I wouldn't think so. People drive themselves crazy, don't they? Something working on the inside that comes out?" He jammed his foot on the brake, turned to look at her. "How come you asked me that?"

She didn't answer him.

Horns blew angrily behind them.

He got the cab moving again. Dark eyes

watching her in the rear view mirror, he said, "There's nothing wrong with you."

"Marty was real," Mickey said thoughtfully. "You saw her, too. The others saw her."

"But that doesn't say she was your sister, you know."

"That's true. And suppose . . . suppose you were right . . . suppose Marty was somebody else, playing a game with me. But then . . . then where is my real twin? If I can't find out about Marty, maybe finding my real twin would at least prove that Marty wasn't . . . ." Mickey took a deep breath. "Listen, Ben, I don't want to go home. Take me to Mrs. Markham's. Remember that first time? The doctor's wife?"

"So you came back," Mrs. Markham grumbled. "I told you I don't know anything about Boris' business."

"I have to keep bothering you," Mickey said apologetically. "But it's so important to me. It's so . . . ."

The old woman's face softened. "I guess it is. If you came back." She stood there, thinking, peering into Mickey's anxious eyes. Finally, shrugging, she said, "Well, maybe. I just hope I'm not sorry. What I don't want is trouble. You understand that? No trouble. Boris didn't want any either. But all right.

You wait. I'll go see." She hobbled into the hall.

Mickey sat waiting, feet together, hands folded in her lap. She counted seconds, then minutes, until she lost track, and it began to seem as if she had been left alone for a very long time.

She jumped up and ran to meet Mrs. Markham as soon as she heard her step in the hall.

Mrs. Markham said, "I did remember." She offered the sheets of stiff paper to Mickey, sheets that had torn along their old folds. "I found it. But it's not good news. Still, you wanted to know . . ."

Mickey, reading what was written on the two sheets, felt the blood drain out of her head. She leaned against the wall, the old woman twittering anxiously, "Are you all right?"

Mickey nodded, bent to read the papers again.

They were both birth certificates. One was for a female child, born 4:30 a.m., six pounds one ounce, named Marion, and giving the mother's name, the father's name. The other was for a male child, born 4:58 a.m., three pounds three ounces, deceased.

She was stunned, knowing now that she had been wrong in believing what she most wanted to believe. Marty had not been her sister. Marty had been an impostor, pretending to be what she could never have been.

Mickey managed to thank Mrs. Markham, to get back to the cab. She gasped the truth out to Ben, and then asked, "But why did she do it? And how could she? How could any stranger know so much about what had happened, about me?"

Ben said, "I've got to tell you what I think. For your father's sake as much as yours. I don't think you ought to go back to Bassett Place. Not ever."

Home.

The whispering voices . . .

The watching eyes . . .

The long and living shadows.

She shuddered, but said, "I have to know the truth. That's where I'll find it."

Theodora was on the phone. "But, Vivian, I can't. You know what Alexander said. Well, how do I know how long?"

Mickey, listening without shame, paused at the top of the stairs.

"I can't help it. I don't know, Vivian," Theodora said after a brief pause.

Mickey, wondering what that was about, came down the steps.

Theodora turned, glanced at her, mumbled, "All right, I'll see about it. Goodbye, Ellen," and hung up, blue eyes filled with guilt watching Mickey. "Pain in the neck," Theodora sighed.

"Who? Vivian?"

Theodora nodded, then flushed. "No. Ellen. I . . ."

"Oh? I thought you were talking to Vivian," Mickey said.

Theodora shrugged, then looked relieved when the front door opened and Alexander came in.

Theodora flounced upstairs.

Alexander suggested that Mickey have dinner with him. "It's been a depressing week," he said.

She didn't want to spend any more time than she had to with him, with any of the Warrens. But she agreed to go, and went to her room to change, still wondering about Vivian's phone call.

Alexander took Mickey to the Occidental. They had a small round table near the piano, and during the meal the smiling violinist lingered near them, playing romantic songs.

Alexander's plump face grew pink and intense, and Mickey, trying to avoid his ardent blue eyes, carefully studied the hundreds of framed and autographed pictures that covered the restaurant walls.

She thought she had settled once and for all Alexander's suggestion that she consider his proposal of marriage. Yet she wasn't really surprised when he said, "Mickey, you do remember how I feel about you, don't you?"

"We've settled that, Alexander."

"A man can dream . . . hope, can't he?"

She thought of Vivian then, and put her suspicion into words. "Alexander, wasn't there something between you and Vivian?"

His blue eyes narrowed. "We were once engaged," he said stiffly. "I ought to have told you before. But . . ."

"Never mind," Mickey said.

Alexander and Vivian had been engaged . . . He had broken that engagement, and begun to court Mickey. Somehow the thought of it frightened her.

Now there was an odd look on his face, a familiar one. It took her a moment to recognize it. But then memory came flooding back.

Alexander was thirteen then and she was seven.

He, at the top of the steps, blocked the way. She, at the bottom, pleaded to be let by, and finally wept.

Winifred, white-haired, apparently the same age then as now, surged out of the house. She grabbed Alexander by the shoulders, shook him hard. "You are not to do that. You are to let Mickey alone. You're Bassett born and bred, but you're here on sufferance. Do you understand me? On sufferance. Now apologize!"

Alexander looked at Mickey, looked down at her for a long full moment. Icy blue eyes spoke rage repressed. Round pink cheeks froze with menace.

Mickey had completely forgotten that incident until she had seen the expression on Alexander's face when she told him that his relationship with Vivian didn't matter to Mickey herself.

Now he said, as if that odd expression had not crossed his face, as if, indeed, she hadn't answered him at all, "You need someone to take care of you. Bennett thought so, too. And surely, after what's happened . . ."

But Alexander didn't know what had happened. He knew nothing of the notes, the phone calls, the flowers. He knew nothing of false Marty, nor of the boy who had been Mickey's twin so long before.

Or did he know?

He said, "You do at least see how delicate you are. Since that unfortunate girl died . . ."

"There's nothing wrong with me, Alexander. You know it. And I know it."

"My dear, you can hardly deny . . ."

She said stiffly, "You won't talk me into it, Alexander."

He raised his pale brows. "Talk you into

what, Mickey?"

She didn't answer him.

But she thought of Noah, the mockery in bottomless dark eyes in which, when she looked incautiously, she felt that she might drown.

Alexander gave her a forced smile. "You really refuse to accept what we could be to each other, Mickey?"

"I will not marry you," she said. She turned her gaze from the hot, burning look of his eyes. "The music is lovely, isn't it?"

"Very," he said shortly, "if you like that kind of thing."

She was relieved that he suggested very soon that since she looked so tired, they should return home.

Winifred was still up.

She smiled at Mickey, at Alexander; she smiled so expectantly, that Mickey, saying good-night, and going upstairs, wondered if Winifred and Alexander had discussed the proposal of marriage together, if Winifred had been waiting, hoping, to hear happy news of a betrothal.

It was the next day.

Mickey sat in the big chair before the dormer window, hands clasped in her lap. The diamonds in her engagement ring, her wedding ring, winked at her like malevolent eyes.

She knew that she must not behave as if she were still entitled to live in the cocoon of that excessively prolonged childhood which Bennett had made possible. "Mayfield's theorem," he said lightly, but meaning it. "There is no way to resolve doubt but to search for certainty."

Yet every step she had taken led to further confusion, fear, doubt. Had led to . . . death.

Runyon . . .

Marty . . .

And deaths come in threes, Mickey reminded herself.

Who then would be next?

But she knew the answer.

She must be the third victim.

She saw now faint outlines of a pattern in everything that had happened since she returned to Bassett Place.

That first night, Noah had been there, waiting in the dark, dozing, he said. He had seen her fright, told her that she mustn't stay in the house, reminded her of her illness.

Noah . . . whose very touch was the memory of sweetness. Whose touch, long before the one time he had kissed her, had always been sweetness. Whose bottomless dark eyes, searching hers that day in the Copenhagen garden, had brought her to the moment of compelling closeness she never forgot. And Bennett, coming out to help her with the flowers, had known that. It was just because he sensed the attraction between Noah and Mickey, that Bennett had said Noah must some day grow up.

But that first night, Noah had been there. The phone calls began, the notes, the flowers.

But Winifred had been there, too.

Winifred . . . obsessed with the Bassett name, and with the Bassett fortune.

Theodora . . . hinting for a new convertible.

And Alexander . . . first helpful, affectionate, then insistently courting her. Alexander, who had been engaged to Vivian — when was the engagement broken? — telling someone on the phone not to call him at the house, being annoyed to find Vivian there, and relieved when she left. And Vivian herself . . . looking angrily at Mickey.

Alexander, courting her so insistently that he was jealous of his own brother, jealous of Noah, who had said, "The two Warren brothers have lost their heads for love of you," and then said, "I thought I would give you time, but since Alexander is pressing his suit . . ." Alexander, who refused to accept her rejection of him, who seemed to resent her wanting to see her father's papers, but had at last, given her some of them. And among them, the letter from Dr. Markham about the twins. Had Alexander known that letter was there? Had he deliberately led her to Marty Plainard?

Winifred had known that Mickey had had a twin. Had she also known that twin was dead? Winifred had eyed Alexander's suit with approval, with hope, and was never happy to see Vivian Starr.

Mickey saw faint outlines of a pattern.

The Bassett fortune, Bassett Place, rose like an iceberg in a sea of uncertainty.

The Bassett fortune . . . Mickey got to her feet, the decision made. She must see the rest of her father's papers.

But she would not ask Alexander to bring them home to her. She would not suffer the excuses, the delays, he would apologetically arrange. Instead, she would go to his office.

She took a warm coat from her closet, and went downstairs.

Theodora had just come in. "It's getting cold." She shuddered, hugging her furs to her. "What I need is something new . . . something beautiful."

Mickey ignored the hint. She called Ben, and a few minutes later, he picked her up. "Everything all right?" he asked.

She nodded. A grown-up didn't blurt out

wild suspicions. She couldn't tell him what she was thinking. She didn't want to admit her fear.

Runyon.

Marty.

She herself . . .

When she went into Alexander's office, the receptionist gave her a startled look, "Hey . . . that's funny. You look an awful lot like somebody I used to know."

Mickey's lips went dry. She asked, in a near whisper, "Like Marty? Marty Plainard?"

The receptionist was bright-eyed, pink-checked, apologetic. "Well, yes . . . but just for a minute . . . I mean . . ."

"But how did you know Marty?"

"Oh, she used to work here. She quit a while back. Going to make a pile of money she said. And then look what happened to her!"

Mickey wanted to turn, to run away from the quick words.

Marty had worked in Alexander's office.

Alexander had known her, but pretended not to.

Mickey had had to identify Marty's still face, to give her name, while all along Alexander had known who she was.

Before Mickey could collect her thoughts, Alexander came out of the inner office. He said quickly, "Oh, I didn't know you were here. Come in. Come inside."

And yet, there was something in his voice, something that told her he at last accepted the fact that she had meant her refusal of his unwanted proposals. There was something in his voice that warned her, threatened her.

There was a painting on the wall. Seeking for diversion, she mentioned it.

"That's one of Noah's." Alexander shrugged. "I bought it as a favor, took it off his hands."

She remembered then that Noah sometimes worked for Alexander, worked in the office. Noah, too, must have known Marty. Noah could have . . .

"Now," Alexander asked, "I presume you came in for a reason?"

She explained that she wanted to see the rest of her father's papers.

Alexander immediately got two large envelopes from the files.

She rose to leave, but he delayed her, saying, "There are a great many more, you know. Shall I bring the rest home with me?"

"I'll work through these first, thank you."

He sighed. "I hope you weren't waiting a long time before I came out and found you. You can't imagine what trouble I have getting decent help. They come and go so fast I hardly get to know them."

She made some pointless, sympathetic comment and left quickly.

She wondered if he had heard what the receptionist had told her about Marty Plainard, if he were letting her know that Marty could have worked for him without his realizing it.

Mickey found it difficult to believe that he could think he could convince her of that.

15

She pushed the papers aside. There was nothing in them to answer her questions. Nothing except the facts of the substance her father had left her.

Her mind went back to the bright-eyed, pink-cheeked receptionist in Alexander's office.

Marty had once worked for him.

Alexander must have known her.

Noah probably had known her.

Marty quit her job, told several people that she expected to get a lot of money soon.

Marty had called Mickey, left her notes, sent her flowers, clothes. And then, suddenly, Marty had spoken to Mickey directly, but that was only after Mickey had decided that Marty must be her long-lost twin. Marty had been startled then, frightened and thoughtful. She'd promised to meet Mickey and hadn't, until on that very last day she'd said, "It's more complicated than you think," and finally agreed.

Marty pretending to be Mickey's twin sister, first only an unknown presence, then a giggle, and finally a voice that demanded,

"You know me?" in bewildered surprise. And so soon after, Marty was dead.

Shadowy outlines in a pattern.

No more than that.

Mickey straightened the papers, put them into their envelopes. She might as well return them to Alexander.

The house was wrapped in twilight silence.

She wondered where everyone had gone.

Suddenly the silence shattered on the quick repeated ring of the downstairs doorbell.

She waited for a moment, expecting that Bevis would answer it.

The shrill harsh peal paused, then stroked through the stillness again.

Mickey got up slowly. Bevis must have gone back to the apartment over the garage.

Mickey didn't really want to answer the door, to see who was there. It didn't matter to her. Whoever waited at the door could go, or stay, forever. There was no one she wanted to see.

No one. No one.

The depression weighed on her, ugly, cold, frightening.

Yet she was drawn downward, her unwilling feet moving from step to step.

She thought of her life with Bennett, secure, sweet. All goodness. The horror had begun when Bennett died. The horror had begun when Bennett died, and she returned to Bassett Place.

When her parents died, Bennett had taken care of everything for her. She had not had to concern herself with the Bassett fortune. She had not even imagined coming home. She never thought of the valley of long and living shadows. Her life with Bennett was supposed to go on forever. But nine months later . . . just nine months, soon after the Warrens had visited them, Bennett was gone, and she was a widow — a widow, grieving and alone — and somehow shamed that there had been a moment in the garden when she felt for another man what she had never felt for Bennett.

She had had no one to turn to except the Warrens.

She had come home, and the horror began.

When Bennett died . . .

The words echoed, loud, then louder, until they made a rhythm for the pounding of her heart.

She froze on the stairs, clung to the bannister.

She wondered if she were wandering, blindfolded, in the valley of the long and living shadow. She wondered if she had lost her mind. The words echoed . . . When Bennett died . . .

Could he have been murdered?

Bennett?

Runyon?

Martha?

But Bennett had had a heart attack. The doctor knew about it, even though Mickey herself had never known, never guessed that he was ill.

A heart attack . . .

Suppose someone else had guessed Bennett's true condition.

Winifred had warned Mickey that he didn't look well.

The others might have realized that something was wrong.

Alexander, Theodora, Noah . . . all of them had visited in the Copenhagen house.

The doctor knew of Bennett's condition, would assume if anything happened that Bennett's heart had given out.

Alexander, Bennett once said laughing, even wrote letters at Bennett's desk.

Noah, Mickey remembered, sat there, swinging his leg.

Theodora had preferred that room above all others in which to study the store catalogs, and Winifred . . .

Bennett had kept his pills in the desk.

She could see the bottle, see it just as it looked when she found it after his death.

She still had the same bottle of pills. She had never been able to throw it away.

Surely, if someone, but who? Who? If someone had put something, a poison, into those pills, with them, there would be a sign, a remainder, some proof left.

But no one had been there, no one except she herself, the day Bennett died.

She seized on that objection, ready to accept it, ready to believe that she must be wrong.

But instantly she knew how it could have been done. If only a few of the pills had been tampered with, months might have passed before the plot was successful, before Bennett took the poisoned pills and died.

But was it possible to poison pills? Or to make poison look like medication? Was there some way of checking the pills that remained?

There must be.

Someone would know where, how, it could be done.

She drew a long slow breath, heartsick, frightened, and went on down the steps, even though she realized that for several moments she hadn't heard the ringing of the doorbell.

She knew, as soon as she reached the hall, that she needn't open the door.

Breath frozen, gray eyes wide, she stared at the threshold.

A familiar white envelope lay there.

Her hand trembled as she bent to pick it up.

She opened it, knowing what she would find.

The black ink printed in heavy bat tracks across the white page.

The familiar words.

I know you. But you don't know me.

But Marty was dead.

Marty, impostor, false twin, couldn't have written that frightening message.

If she hadn't written that one, then she had written none of them.

But someone had, the same someone who stole a car and ran her down on the street outside of Bassett Place.

The same someone who had schemed with her, paid her to call Mickey, to send the flowers, the clothes.

But who?

Who killed Bennett so that Mickey would return home?

Who killed Marty to keep her from moving into the house as Mickey's twin?

And Runyon? Who had killed Runyon? Why? Why had Runyon died?

Mickey, clasping the note, fled back to the safety of her room, hid it among her father's papers.

Why had the notes begun again?

When would the phone start to ring again?

What did that mean?

She didn't know, but she had to find out.

The question was where to begin, how.

That night at dinner, with the candlelight gleaming in her white hair, Winifred said, "Mickey dear child, you are so quiet. You must try harder not to dwell too much on the past, you know. It isn't good for you. It isn't safe."

The uneven modulation, stressing some words and not others, seemed to convey whole categories of unexpressed meanings.

Mickey considered them for only a moment before she said, "It's the present that I'm thinking about, Aunt Winifred."

"The present, dear?"

"Yes. The present. And myself."

"That is . . ." Winifred hesitated. "I'm afraid that is not quite clear."

"There are some things . . . things that I never mentioned to any of you."

Alexander asked sharply, "What do you mean? What things?"

She forced herself to go on. "You always asked me how I found Marty. Well, actually, she found me."

Winifred gasped. "But, really, Mickey . . ."

"Just a minute, Mother," Alexander cut in.

"Don't you think you should allow Mickey to explain all this?"

"It sounds crazy to me," Theodora announced.

"Theodora . . ." Winifred gave Mickey an apologetic look. "She didn't mean that, of course."

Mickey went on, "It does sound funny, but Marty found me. The first night of my arrival home, there was a note near the door. Then there were phone calls, but nobody spoke to me when I answered."

"Do you realize what you're saying, Mickey?" Alexander demanded, his pink pudgy face full of concern.

"Of course." She met his steady gaze. "Alexander, Marty used to work for you."

"For me?"

Mickey nodded.

"That's absurd."

"Is it?" Mickey shrugged. "Notes, phone calls, flowers, clothes. And then, among my father's papers, I found the letter from Dr. Markham about the expected twins. So I was sure that it was my twin trying to reach me. And when she called again, I told her so, and I begged her to meet me. She did meet me, and she promised to come here. And before she did, she was killed."

Winifred moaned, "Mickey, my poor child

. . . all this that has happened . . . you must try . . ."

Theodora raised blue eyes to the ceiling. "What a story!"

Alexander said, "Go on, Mickey, you might as well tell us the rest of this . . . this . . ."

"Marty was not my twin."

"But of course not . . . we all tried to tell you," Winifred said.

"She couldn't have been," Mickey went on steadily. "I know that for certain now. My twin was a boy, Aunt Winifred. A boy. And he was dead at birth."

"Extraordinary," Winifred murmured.

"So Marty was an impostor. And she died. But the notes have begun again. And soon the phone calls will!"

There was a long empty silence.

At last Alexander said, frowning, "But Mickey, dead people don't send notes. What are you saying?"

"Someone else, not Marty, wrote the notes."

Alexander gave her a disbelieving look.

Winifred made a protesting sound.

Theodora laughed.

Mickey tried to read guilt, to see what lay behind the concealing expressions that each one of them wore.

But it was impossible.

And Noah . . . Noah was not there.

She wished that he were.

She wished he were with her.

She told herself that she wanted to look at his expression, too.

"Notes, phone calls . . ." Alexander shook his head. "Mickey, if you knew what this sounds like . . ."

"I have proof," she reminded him. "The note . . ." She jumped to her feet, hurried upstairs.

She would show them the note.

They would see it, and know that she knew.

The guilty one would understand what it meant.

She reached into her father's papers.

The note wasn't there.

She sat at the desk, turned each sheet over carefully, read each page. She shook the sheaf out, looked under the desk, around it. She searched her room. At last she had to admit it to herself. The note was gone.

All proof of the barely glimpsed pattern was gone.

In that instant, she knew why Runyon had been killed.

He had seen the notes, knew about the phone calls. He was a witness to what was happening to her. So he had died.

She shivered.

Runyon because he knew what was happening.

Marty because she knew too much.

There was a sound at the door. Mickey spun around.

Bevis stared at her. "Listen, they want to know. Are you all right? Are you coming down? Coffee's ready."

Mickey nodded.

She didn't want to return to the dining room, but she knew she would have to tell them some time.

She went downstairs. As she neared the dining room, she heard Winifred say, "This is terrifying. I can hardly believe . . ."

Alexander answered, "Don't get upset. It's going to be all right."

"Maybe it will," Theodora laughed. "But she sure won't. She's really gone round the bend."

"But the whole thing," Winifred protested. "I mean . . ."

"Mother, don't you see what's happening to Mickey," Alexander demanded. "Don't you understand? She can't help it. I'm sure she doesn't really mean all this. We just have to . . ."

Mickey went in, her face pale, haggard, her lips dry with fear.

"Well, Mickey?" Alexander asked.

"The note's gone," she whispered.

There was another moment of empty silence.

Then Winifred cried, "Gone? But how can it be gone, Mickey dear. If you had it, read it, how can it have disappeared?"

"Someone took it," Mickey said, her gray eyes moving from Winifred's face to Alexander's, then on to Theodora's.

"That's ridiculous," Winifred said quietly. "How on earth can you imagine . . . who would do such a . . ."

Alexander cut in, "You're sure you had a note?"

"Of course."

"But you can't show it to us."

"I told you," she said.

"Drink your coffee, dear," Winifred cried. "Never mind. Just forget it for now. We'll forget it, too. Such a to-do over nothing . . . really, dear, calm down."

Alexander rose. He paced the floor, two steps one way, two another. His plump face was red. His blue eyes seemed to shoot angry sparks at Mickey.

"Mickey, I've hesitated to say this, but as your lawyer, entrusted by Bennett to look after you, as your cousin, even as the man who loves you though I realize now that I must accept being rejected by you — as all these, I must tell you that your behavior, for some time now, has been so strange that I . . . well, I've been wondering . . ."

"I'm perfectly all right, Alexander," she said quietly, though her voice shook.

"You're perfectly all right," he retorted, his voice heavy with irony. "Look at yourself in the mirror. You're as pale as a ghost. Your hands are shaking. You seem ready to fall to pieces at any moment. You go off, pick up some strange girl, God knows where, decide she is your sister. You say I once employed her. Perhaps. Perhaps not. I didn't recognize the name, nor the face. Believe me or not, as you chose. Noah, who often works for me, didn't seem to recognize her either. When she dies, you cry out 'Murder.' Yes, that's what you were insisting. You embarrass us before the police, everyone. Just as you did with Runyon. A total exhibition of yourself . . . yes, I'm sorry, Mickey. But it's true. And now . . . now you're talking about notes. Notes that don't exist. That never did. You're hardly competent. I'm afraid — we all are — of what you'll do next."

Hardly competent, she thought.

But it had all happened. It was true, not imagined.

Bennett had died, and Runyon, and Marty . . .

The note had been real.

She said, "I'm not sure . . . I don't know what you mean, Alexander."

He answered more gently, "If you don't try, dear, don't settle down, begin to behave like a rational person . . ."

Winifred protested, "Really, Alexander, I think you are needlessly frightening Mickey." She went on, her lined, powdered face as expressionless as always, "Now, Mickey, dear, do have your coffee, and then go upstairs. Lie down, have a bit of a rest. All this . . ."

"There was no note," Alexander said firmly. "Now get that into your head while you're having your rest."

She shielded her eyes, looking down into her cup. She took it into her hand, held it steadily, carefully, and drank three long swallows of the very bitter, very strong black coffee. It seemed to clear her head. She emptied the cup quickly and put it down.

Alexander had known all along who Marty was. He could have put her up to pretending to be Mickey's twin.

And Noah . . . yes . . . Noah had worked around Alexander's office at different times.

Winifred had always known about the twins, and was intent on the Bassett fortune, the Bassett name. She could have met Marty at some time or other.

Even Theodora might have met Marty in Alexander's office.

Any of them, or all of them, could be responsible for everything that had happened.

Why?

Hardly competent, Alexander had said.

Change that to incompetent.

And he was a lawyer.

How easy for him, with the others helping him, to have her declared insane.

A black haze shifted before her eyes.

Or was she?

Once, long before, she had walked in the valley of shadows.

Was all that had happened no more than a dream?

Mickey raised frightened eyes, looked around the table. They were all watching her. She saw nothing but bewilderment, anxiety, in their faces.

Winifred reproached her, "How can you think that anyone would . . . would play such a prank on you, poor child."

"If you would only see a doctor," Alexander told her gravely, while Theodora nodded in agreement.

Mickey got to her feet. "I would prefer that you keep your worry about me to yourself," she said bitterly. "If you are really worried.

I will manage very well on my own, I assure you."

Noah, lounging in the doorway, shouted, "Bravo, Mickey," and laughed.

She turned, looked at him, wavering on her feet.

She hadn't heard him come in, didn't know until he spoke that he was there.

He came toward her, lithe, as graceful as a tiger, his bottomless dark eyes burning. "Mickey, what is it?"

"You . . . all of you . . ." she gasped, "you're trying to drive me insane."

He caught her arm, shook her hard.

Oddly, she was aware, even then, of a sweetness in his touch. She felt as if she were drowning in his compelling gaze.

She pushed him away, fled past him, tripped and stumbled past Bevis, and flung herself up the stairs.

She awakened suddenly.

There had been a sound.

But now, listening, she heard nothing.

She was sure there had been a whisper. She told herself that it might have been no more than something remembered from a dream.

It had taken her a long time to fall asleep.

She kept thinking of Noah, even though she had thrust him away, thrust him away physically, and in her mind as well. But that momentary sweetness in his touch remained with her. She reminded herself that it had been he who first reminded her of the memories of Bassett Place. The tinkle of the chandelier, the scent of rich flowers, the drifting cigarette smoke, and Noah, rising up in the darkness. They made her think of the living shadow.

He had worked for Alexander, and could so easily have met Marty there. And then . . . ?

He had made her love him. Yes, yes, she must admit it to herself. He had made her love him. The compelling sweetness must be love. Was it for herself? Or for the Bassett fortune?

She fell asleep, saying his name, and now awake she thought his name. She made herself stop. She tried to listen.

The house whispered as always, but beyond the whisper, her straining ears heard the sound again.

She moved as if hypnotized. She snatched a robe, slippers. She went swiftly, moving on tiptoe, into the hall.

There was nothing. Nothing.

Yet she was drawn down, drawn through the dark to the second floor.

Tiptoeing still, quick, light, silent, she ran down the steps.

The lower hall was empty, still.

She paused at the top of the second flight, listening and frightened, yet unable to turn back, unable to cry out.

There was no time for her to brace herself. She had no warning.

From somewhere behind her there was a rush of movement.

Black bat wings hovering at the edge of her consciousness?

She didn't know. She didn't know.

Then the rush of movement became a great hard thrusting blow.

It flung her forward, tumbling into the empty dark.

16

She fell heavily, a wild scream torn from her throat.

The shadows reached up from her through spinning emptiness. A void without end. A great, wrenching pain that struck through her on waves of brilliance, and then an instant of sudden safety, of comfort, in reaching arms.

In that instant, as she looked up into Noah's face, lit by the chandelier's glow, she foundered in impermanent elation, she knew that love might have a murderer's name, but it was still love. Noah was love.

It was an impermanent elation, and lasted only a moment.

Then the memory of the great thrusting blow, the spinning fall through emptiness, the wrenching pain out of which Noah's arms had scooped her, returned.

He was demanding, hoarse, frightened, "Mickey, are you all right? What happened?"

"Somebody pushed me down the steps," she gasped.

"Pushed you, Mickey?"

She didn't know, couldn't tell, if it was fear, or disbelief, or mockery, that shuttered his bottomless dark eyes.

"Mickey, what are you talking about?"

She winced as he drew her closer. "My arm, Noah."

He held her more gently, looking into her face. "Now. Slowly. Tell me what really happened."

She still couldn't read his bottomless eyes. She didn't know what to say.

And at the same time from above, from the second floor, there came more light, and voices, both suddenly spilling down the stairs.

Alexander appeared on the landing. He wore a robe. His blond hair was tousled. "What's going on?" he demanded irritably, yawning still. "What's the noise about?"

Past his shoulder, Mickey saw Winifred. She, too, was in a robe, purple velvet, as luxurious as a court gown. The white hair was piled high still, and gleamed in the pink light. The firm chin was more firm in a chin strap. As she peered down at Mickey, Winifred seemed to remember the chin strap, for with a quick furtive motion, she snatched it off and asked, "What happened, dear child. Why are you up at this hour?"

Alexander glared from the landing. "Is this a proper way to behave?" His blue eyes were narrowed in suspicion.

The first shock, the numbness, the elation

of love, were wearing off now. Mickey felt chill enwrap her in an aching shawl. She rose, moving from within the false protection of Noah's encircling arms.

She looked first at Noah, then at Winifred and Alexander. Behind them, she saw Theodora sidle into the light.

She said very slowly, very distinctly, "Someone pushed me down the stairs."

Winifred gasped and surged toward the first floor, purple robe flowing behind her.

"What?" Alexander yelled. "Pushed you? Who? Who could have pushed you, Mickey?" He was so close behind his mother that he very nearly trod on the purple velvet.

Theodora collapsed at the top of the steps, a plump wraith in pink net, with giant curlers torturing her blond hair.

"Who?" Alexander demanded again.

Noah echoed it, but softly, gently, "Who, Mickey?"

"What's that she said?" Winifred was demanding. "What was it, Mickey? Someone pushed you? Why, my dear child . . . but no one . . . no one in this house . . ." Winifred looked around helplessly. "Noah, what are you doing here? I thought you left hours and hours ago."

"I was sitting on the porch. Thinking, I guess you'd call it." Noah still held Mickey, and it was to her that he said, "But this time it didn't put me to sleep. Though I might as well have been."

From the top of the stairs, Theodora said languidly, "I still don't know what all the fuss is about. Mickey's always saying something crazy, isn't she?"

Noah looked down at Mickey. If he had heard Theodora, he had no reaction to her words. He said, "Let's see your arm. At the moment, I'm more interested in how you are than in what happened."

"My arm's all right," she said, thinking that she was more interested in what had happened, who had pushed her, than in how she was. Did Noah actually know what had happened? Was that why he didn't care about that? She wondered.

"No. Look here." He touched her wrist, her fingers. The slim bones seemed to have doubled in size. The flesh was full, and tight. At his touch, light as it was, a nauseating wave of sickness launched on pain flooded through her.

She gasped, light fading as her breath failed her.

"It could be broken," Noah said. He turned Mickey, turned her on melting legs, toward the door. "Come on. I'll take you out to Sibley. We'll have it X-rayed right now."

Alexander sputtered, "Noah, will you wait a minute? I must know what's going on here."

"Mickey fell down the steps," Noah retorted, his lean face blank, his words spaced evenly and underscored with barely controlled anger. "She fell in the dark, and she may have broken her wrist. What else do you think you have to know right now?"

There was a brief silence.

Into it, Mickey said softly, "I didn't fall, Noah. I told you. I was pushed. Somebody came up behind me and shoved me, and . . ."

"You see?" Alexander was triumphant. "How can you take her to the hospital when she talks like that? Look at her. What will they think? We can't expose her to that."

Mickey turned her head slightly.

From the big, gold-framed mirror, a small girl peered at her — a small girl with wild black curls, with wild gray eyes, with a trembling mouth. A small girl who looked quite mad.

Was she mad?

Had she come up out of sleep with love on her lips and thought of murder?

Had she heard a sound in the night? Or had that been a dream, too?

Had Bennett, and Runyon, and Marty died?

Or was she lost in the valley of long and living shadows?

Mickey whimpered, clinging to what she remembered. "I was pushed, I tell you."

Noah slipped an arm around her shoulder. "It's going to be all right."

Winifred said thoughtfully, "Why, Alexander, there's nobody here but us. Right now, I mean. But do you think . . . I mean perhaps before . . . a burglar. Someone in to loot the house . . . we haven't looked after all." Her speculative eyes, the color of grayish-brown ice, were on Mickey's taut face.

"There was someone," Mickey told her.

Alexander answered begrudgingly, "Well, of course, there might have been." He swung away. "Come on, Mother, let's have a look around." And to Noah, "Just a minute."

But Noah, as soon as Alexander and Winifred had gone into the living room, called up to Theodora, "Get a blanket, will you?"

She disappeared, returning quickly to fling a fleecy white blanket down the steps.

It came tumbling, limp, helpless, to fall into the hall.

Mickey, watching it, shuddered.

Noah wrapped it around her, lifted her into his arms, ignoring her protests, and carried her out.

As they crossed the threshold, Mickey heard Alexander yell, "Noah, wait. I'll take her."

Noah swore under his breath, then grinned

at Mickey. "Sorry, but my brother can annoy me." Sobering, he asked, "Hurt much?" as he eased her into the car.

"Not now."

"Hold steady when we go around corners, O.K.?"

She nodded.

As they drove under the gaslights, she caught a glimpse of his face. It was shadow-marked, somehow grim.

And it was then that he asked, "Mickey, do you know, are you certain, that you were pushed?"

She knew he was watching her. She gave him a defiant "Yes!"

"Who did it, Mickey?"

She wondered if he had asked that question too quickly.

She wondered why he had still been at the house?

"Or . . ." his voice went very deep, "are you afraid to tell me?"

"I don't know who it was. There was only the dark. Then I just felt a movement behind me, felt it and heard it. It turned into a hard push. It threw me off balance."

"I was outside, sitting on the porch. I heard you scream, and got inside, and hit the light switch. You were still falling then. It seemed like slow motion to me. And Mickey, I didn't see anybody at the top of the stairs."

She closed her eyes, trying to remember exactly how it had been.

She was falling. She hit something — a step? the bannister? the wall? There was pain, and sudden light. And then she was in Noah's arms.

Could time have deceived her as she spun through the dark?

Could he have been on the second floor, somewhere behind her, and reached from the shadows to push her down? Could he have come down so quickly himself that he was able to turn on the chandelier, hold her for that sweet instant? Or, could he, moving with that swift tigerish grace, have dropped over the bannister so lightly that she didn't hear him?

The door . . . she didn't remember hearing the door open, close. Yet, when Noah carried her out, the door had definitely been closed. She remembered how he had fumbled to open it while she buried her face in his shoulder.

She slid a sideways look at him, and caught his dark eyes watching her again.

Was he wondering if she believed what he had told her, she asked herself.

She said, "You were still on the porch. It's the middle of the night, Noah."

"I sat down to do some thinking." He gave

her another side glance. "About what I walked in on tonight."

She didn't answer him, though he paused, obviously waiting for her to say something.

"I'd like to know what they had been doing to you, Mickey, what they had been saying."

She wished that she could believe him. But she didn't remember at what moment he had appeared in the doorway behind her to say, "Bravo, Mickey," and laugh, then to ask, bottomless eyes burning, "Mickey, what is it?"

She didn't know what he had heard of the things she told the rest of the family. But she knew she had said too much then. Some one among the Warrens had listened to her, and made plans. Her fall through the dark was the result.

"Mickey?" Noah asked.

She sighed. "I'm tired."

"Sorry. Catch your breath now. We'll talk later on."

But she did not want to talk.

She had already said too much.

She was to be the third victim.

Runyon, Marty, and now . . .

Bennett . . . her thoughts went back to him. It had begun then, when he died. And she still had the pills . . .

Noah pulled into the parking lot, stopped at the emergency entrance, helped her inside.

The signing-in, the X-rays, took only moments, for which she was grateful.

There was no break, only a bad sprain in her left wrist. It was bound and taped. A small cut over her left temple, unnoticed by anyone until then, was cleaned and taped, too.

They were soon on the way back to the house, Mickey, silent, wrapped in the blanket Noah had tucked carefully around her.

He finally said, "It's lucky it wasn't worse."

She didn't answer him.

He said thoughtfully, "It might be a good idea if you took a trip, got away for a little while."

She thought of leaving the house, its whispering voices, watching eyes. She thought of the quick hot fear which had enwrapped her since her return home.

Strangely, she realized that she had left that fear behind her. She could not imagine the valley of long and living shadows. Her doubt was gone into certainty. She was secure in her sanity. Bennett had been right.

She didn't know when she had stepped out of the boundaries of that old nightmare. It might have been when she cried, "You're trying to drive me mad," offering that dangerous challenge to the one Warren who would act on it. Or it might have been when she felt the sudden thrust in the dark, the spinning fall that ended in Noah's arms.

She was out of the valley of long and living shadows. But the fear that had once been fear of herself was now the fear of someone unknown. And if she left Bassett Place, if she didn't discover the truth about Bennett, if Runyon's death, and Marty's went unexplained, then, Mickey knew, she would herself bear a new burden of fear forever.

"It would be a good idea," Noah said. "Think about it."

"I can't go away now," she told him.

"But I don't think it's good for you to live with the family. I didn't like it in the beginning. I like it less now."

"I meant what I said tonight."

"I realize that."

She rather hoped that Noah would tell the other Warrens that they ought to leave Bassett Place. Let them go, and she would feel safer, but she would still seek and find the truth.

He said gently, as if he could read her thoughts, "There are some things that you have to do for yourself."

She wondered if she could ever summon the strength to face down Winifred's steamroller concern, Alexander's pomposity, Theodora's plaintiveness.

They were all waiting, with coffee ready

and brandy poured, when Mickey and Noah returned.

Winifred cried, "My dear child, you were hurt. What a terrible accident."

"Are you better now?" Alexander demanded.

"Did you break your wrist?" Theodora asked interestedly.

"It was a sprain." Noah looked at Alexander. "Did you find anything when you looked around?"

"Nothing," Alexander snorted. "And I didn't really expect to." His sharp blue eyes focused on Mickey's thin face. "You must have had a bad dream."

She didn't answer him.

Winifred said, "But there was a window open in the living room. It is possible . . ." She smiled at Mickey. "There now, dear, don't worry about it so. It is possible that someone did get into the grounds, prowl through the house a bit. I've checked the silver, of course. There's nothing missing. And I looked among my jewels. All is well there. So . . ." She shrugged, "the best thing to do is forget it, don't you think so, dear?"

Mickey agreed.

She knew that she had to wait until she had proof, had found the truth, before she could do anything but agree.

★ ★ ★

The pills, carefully wrapped in a handkerchief, were in her purse. She took it downstairs with her.

She was made up, her hair brushed and shining. Her suit was pearl gray wool, one that Bennett had bought her in Magasin du Nord when they first arrived in Copenhagen after their honeymoon. She was pleased with the effect of the white frill of blouse that curled under her chin.

It had taken her a long time to manage the many small movements that made up her toilette. It was a job for two hands, when she could only use one. But at least her taped left wrist was no longer painful.

She glanced at the threshold near the front door.

No. There was no small white note lying there.

She wondered how soon she would find one, find one only to have it disappear once again.

From the dining room, she heard the sound of voices.

She went in.

Winifred said, "Good morning, dear. How are you today? And your wrist? You do seem so much better."

Alexander smiled at her, jocular, nearly

233

teasing. "It's hard to believe that you had such a nightmare just a few hours ago."

Theodora grinned at her. "Is that a Saks suit?"

And Noah, watching her over the rim of his coffee cup, said nothing, absolutely nothing, his gaze thoughtful.

She allowed Alexander to draw back a chair for her.

She nodded her thanks, then said, "I'm fine now."

Bevis came in, pink hair wild, plump face suspicious, and served her coffee.

Winifred passed her a silver tray of toast. "You must eat something, dear. I insist. I really do insist."

Mickey looked from one to another of the faces around her, relieved that they were willing to pretend nothing out of the way had happened, wondering if any of them suspected that she had changed, and no longer feared herself.

She answered their comments about the weather, agreeing that it was a cool autumn day. She was noncommittal about her plans for the afternoon, saying she hadn't decided what she would do.

One of them, she knew, or perhaps all of them acting together, hid the hope of murder in his heart.

Some time, and she was certain it would be soon, some time there would be an attempt to make success out of failure.

If she were to save herself she must move quickly.

She had pushed back her chair, preparing to rise. But she saw a suitcase near the door.

Noah said, "That's mine, Mickey. I decided . . . of course you can say 'no' to me . . . but I decided, that if you didn't mind, I'd move in here. There's plenty of room."

His voice went on, even, unexcited, and expressionless, but she didn't hear the rest of his words.

Noah.

He was moving in now.

Instead of relaying her hint that she no longer wanted the Warrens in Bassett Place, he was joining them.

Was it to ensure a more successful attack on her?

Why else should he suddenly give up his own place, his own independence?

"I hope you don't mind," he was saying insistently, his bottomless dark eyes on her face.

In a voice empty, false, to her own ears, she said, "I don't mind, Noah."

"So here we are, all together again," Winifred cried. "Just as we used to be!" Her fond glance moved around the table, dividing an empty smile. "The Bassetts. In Bassett Place."

Alexander said, "I want you to know, Mickey, that we all understand that you were simply upset last night. These odd little things that happened, or might have happened, seemed very important to you then. But we know you didn't mean what you said."

But I did, Mickey thought.

I did mean it. And one of you knows that, too.

17

"Listen," Ben said, tipping his red baseball cap, "listen, are you sure you're all right?"

"I'm all right," she whispered.

"You want me to take you home now?"

"Oh, no!" she cried. "Not yet."

"Then where? Or what about a cup of coffee? Would that help?"

"Could we drive for a little while?"

"Sure we could. And will." He got the cab going, then went on, "How did you hurt your wrist anyhow?"

"I fell down the steps."

"You did?" He waited a moment. "Funny things have happened since you got back. You didn't ask me, but I'm going to tell you what I think. Either you get your hands on them and fix them, or you better get out. But don't just stand still."

"I'm trying to fix them," she said.

"I know you are." His honey-rich voice was reassuring. "You're a brave one, must have been born with it. Only . . . only you're alone. That's what worries me. Your being alone. If I could help . . . if you'd tell me what I could do . . ."

"I'm the only one that can take care of it, Ben. Just me. And I have to do it myself."

The words were an echo of what Noah had once said to her. With his name in her mind, she felt an odd mixture of desire, fright, and shame.

Bennett, smiling in the sunlight of the Copenhagen garden, had seen and recognized what Mickey had not known herself. He had watched Noah and Mickey together. And he had died . . .

The cab turned into M Street, became one of a fleet of cars that rolled along beside the river.

Soon, whistling softly, Ben cut into Canal Road, leaving the traffic behind, and suddenly they were in country.

November bare trees, gray sky, a rising wall of rock at the right.

Somewhere along the way would be Fletcher's Landing where Marty had promised to meet Mickey. Within a mile or two was the dead-end street off MacArthur Boulevard where the car that killed Marty was abandoned.

And also within a mile or two was Bassett Place, the big house surrounded by a tall iron fence, the gates where gaslights flickered in old lamps, and would keep on flickering, Runyon had once told her, as long as Bassett

Place still stands. Runyon had died there, but the gaslights flickered still over the iron gates in the place where it all began.

For the past two days, she had waited, calm in the knowledge of what she would learn, calm even though she knew time was running out for her, knew that one of the Warrens waited, too.

Ben had found the laboratory for her, taken her there. She left the pills, explaining what she wanted.

Now, a few moments ago, she had received her answer.

The young technician said, "You asked that all the pills be analyzed. Right?"

She nodded.

"What was that? Why do you want that information?"

She stared at him, already certain of what he would tell her.

"It isn't really any of my business, of course." He peered at her through rimless glasses that seemed to distort his hazel eyes. "I realize that . . . but . . . you're very young, and . . . I feel . . ."

A stranger was trying to take care of her again, she thought impatiently. The scars of her agonies were all inside. She demanded through dry lips, "What did you find out, please?"

"It could be police business. Most of these pills are just what you'd expect. Nitroglycerin, one of the medications for people suffering from certain heart disorders. But five are . . . " he paused, frowning, then told her the name of a pharmacological preparation of which she had never heard before. At her blank look, he explained, "It's a poison, just about instantly fatal. It leaves few outward symptoms, and those could easily be mistaken for a heart attack, particularly in a person known to have had such a condition."

Then Bennett had been murdered.

She had known it, yet the technician's hesitant words spread an odd numbness through her.

Bennett had been murdered.

Runyon had been murdered.

Marty had been murdered.

The technician was saying that if anything was wrong, if she had any idea . . . she should go to the police.

She fumbled in her bag, paid him and fled.

She knew that he watched her get into the cab.

Ben asked, "Find out what you want?" and looked worried when she said that she had but didn't explain.

Now, driving along the river, she asked herself what she could do. Copenhagen was a long way off. And Bennett had been, as he desired, cremated.

She had pills, among which there were five of poison, but she could never prove that Bennett had taken any of them.

When Runyon fell, the ladder slipping away from him, she said it was no accident. But no one listened to her.

When Marty died, the police ignored Mickey's insistence that Marty had been deliberately run down.

There was no proof. Nothing but an inner certainty of the evil that had been done . . .

Now she saw more clearly the outlines of the pattern.

At her parents' death, in August of the year before, she had become heir to the Bassett fortune. It was that for which someone had waited, and it was then that a well thought-out plan had been set in motion.

She, alone for the first time, suddenly unprotected, with the seed of doubt already in her, must have seemed completely vulnerable.

Winifred had spent three weeks in Copenhagen. She told Mickey that Bennett didn't look well. Was Winifred trying to prepare Mickey for what was to come? Had she slipped poisoned pills into the bottle on the desk? She had known about Mickey's twin, and it must have been that which was the cause of her continuing interest in twins. She had known about Mickey's adoption, and told Mickey of it, and she obviously never quite believed that Mickey had recovered from the breakdown for which Winifred herself could take at least some responsibility. Had what had happened when Mickey was fourteen given Winifred the idea that she could secure the Bassett fortune and Bassett Place, for herself and her children?

When Winifred left, the others arrived. Noah, Theodora, and Alexander. It had been a brief weekend visit, but they had seemed to fill the house.

Theodora obsessed with those things that Mickey took for granted.

Alexander warm and friendly, talking of bonds from the past that Mickey didn't remember.

Noah smiling at her, telling her that she was like a sleeping princess who hadn't awakened, telling her that he hadn't come to Copenhagen to shop or go sight-seeing, but to spend his time with her.

A month later, Bennett was dead.

She returned home, memory full of the valley of long and living shadows, hoping that she was safe, but never sure.

One of them had played upon that uncertainty. One of them had left her the notes, made the calls, sent the flowers and clothes.

Marty Plainard was the instrument through which one of the Warrens worked.

The plan began well, but Mickey had told Runyon about the notes, the calls. He was a witness to her sanity. He had to die.

And when Runyon was dead, Marty had a weapon against the person who had used her. She no longer needed an intermediary, and she could be Mickey's twin, a Bassett, with everything that meant. So Marty had to die.

And with Marty dead, the plot to prove Mickey mad could go on.

There were no witnesses to what had happened.

The notes had been destroyed.

She was quite alone.

And she had spoken in haste. She had cried, "You are trying to drive me mad!"

And so it was time for her to die.

She shivered.

She saw the outlines of the pattern, but she did not see the hand which drew them.

She did not want to return to Bassett Place, yet there was a murderer to be unmasked.

How?

She did not know.

She must wait, as the murderer waited. She must be wary. This was one time when she had to be fearful of an error in making her decision. It was not as simple as giving up the Copenhagen house, although then, she had thought it was the hardest thing she would ever have to do in her life.

She must do nothing, just wait.

Ben said, "Feel like riding a little longer?"

"I guess I might as well go home."

And soon, drawing to a stop before the porch, he asked, "Will you call me? I don't know what's going on. But if you need me . . ."

"I will, Ben."

She slipped out of the cab, paid him, flashed a reassuring smile. "Thanks for everything, Ben."

He frowned at her. "I don't like the sound of that thanks."

She smiled again, and went inside.

She paused before the big mirror to take off her tan beret.

There, propped against the gold frame, was a familiar white note.

She picked it up.

Black bat tracks on the sheet. Yes. Again. *I know you. But you don't know me.*

Once those words had struck terror into her heart. But now she was angry. Another note which would disappear. Soon phone calls that no one but she could speak about. And then . . . ? When she did not tumble, screaming,

244

into madness, when she did not hear whispering voices, see staring eyes, then there would be another sudden blow in the dark. And the Bassett fortune would fall into the hand that had turned against her.

She stuffed the note into her pocket.

She went into the drawing room.

Winifred reared back, her piled-high hair gleaming. "Do come in, dear." She sounded as if Mickey were a bashful guest. "Do come in, and let me pour you tea. You look exhausted. And how's your wrist today?"

"Much better, thanks," Mickey told her, automatic courtesy concealing her anger. Her fingers went to the note in her pocket.

There was no courage in being a willing participant in her own destruction.

She knew what she had to do.

She perched, like a small bird ready for flight, in a deep plush chair.

She said, "Aunt Winifred, I don't want any tea. But I do want to talk to you."

Winifred, busy pouring from the silver pot, paused, looked up, then returned her attention to the Spode cup she had just filled. "My dear, of course. What is it?"

Gently, picking her words, Mickey said, "You've been a great help to me, and I appreciate it. I'm sure you know that. But I feel that we've all made something of a mistake.

It would be better if we were to make our homes separately." She paused, drew a deep breath. "So, as soon as it's convenient . . ."

There. It was done.

She had not been certain, not until she heard the words, that she would have the courage to say them.

"My dear child, I don't understand!" Winifred gasped.

"I'm sorry, Aunt Winifred."

"Now then, dear. We must be honest with each other. Is it because of Noah? Do you find it crowded with him here? For, if so," she gave Mickey an empty smile, "I will take care of that for you. He simply arrived with his suitcase, and there he was. I didn't quite know what to say. I . . ."

Mickey shook her head.

"But why on earth . . . now . . . when we've always lived together . . . The Bassetts, the Warrens. We are your only family."

Bennett had said, "They are all the family you have," and wanted her to be close to them. He felt the need to take care of her, to think of her as surrounded by love. That had been his weakness. So he was murdered.

Runyon had said, "Let me think about it. But it'll be all right." He had wanted to protect her. That had been his weakness. He would have been a witness to her sanity. So he was murdered.

Marty had said, "It's more complicated than you think." She had known too much, and her weakness had been greed. So she was murdered.

Mickey touched the note in her pocket.

Sweet hot anger stirred through her.

She would never forget any of them.

"And Benjamin. Your . . . father. He was always so . . . ."

"Not always," Mickey said. "Remember when I was fourteen."

Winifred cried, "But it was only a misunderstanding. When I . . . you mean you insist we should go? Now? Because of that?"

"Not exactly."

"What then?"

"I'd rather not go into it."

Winifred opened her lightly-painted mouth, shaped soundless words, as Theodora came into the room.

The brief silence seemed to trouble Theodora. She turned her plump face from her mother to Mickey. She asked, "Do you suppose I can have tea?"

No one answered her.

She smoothed her tight green sheath over her round hips, and flung herself into the sofa. "I wish I could have that convertible, Mother.

Really, I don't see why . . ."

"Be quiet," Winifred said.

There was another brief silence.

That time Alexander interrupted it. He stood in the doorway. "All here in time for tea."

"Come in, Alexander." Winifred's voice was shaky, her grayish-brown eyes seemed sunken in brackets of well-powdered wrinkles.

He looked at her, then at Mickey, blue eyes narrowed in a speculative gaze. "What is it?"

"I've had such a terrible shock," Winifred mumbled, the odd modulation of her voice under-playing some words, stressing others, as always. "I don't know what to say, what to think. It seems . . . it seems a terrible nightmare."

Mickey thought, watching Winifred, that Winifred seemed deeply shaken, deeply hurt. Surely only an innocent person could act that way.

Yet how could she be certain, Mickey asked herself.

"What's happened now?" Alexander looked at Mickey, impatience scoring his plump face. He seemed to be thinking, 'Now what have you done?'

"Mickey . . . after all we've done for her, all our effort, and our love, everything . . .

she's just told me that we must leave Bassett Place," Winifred explained.

"But that's crazy!" Theodora cried. "We live here!"

Alexander silenced her with a sour look, turned to Mickey, pompous as always, "And may I ask why you have made such a decision?"

"I think it would be best, Alexander."

"Can you manage alone?"

"I'm sure I can," she said quietly.

"You don't realize what you're saying," Winifred cried. "Don't you remember how it was before we moved in with you? Don't you remember . . ."

Mickey didn't answer.

Alexander asked, "What brought on this sudden change of heart, Mickey?"

"It's what I want."

"And what you want, you must have," Winifred said bitterly. She heaved out of her chair, went to the bell rope, and gave it an angry tug.

In a moment, Bevis came in. "You want more tea?"

"I want you to go to the apartment, Bevis." Without looking at Mickey, Winifred went on, "Yes, fortunately, I do still have the apartment. You'll be sad to hear I will not have to move out on the street . . . me . . . a Bassett.

To be treated this way." Then, to frowning Bevis, "Go to the apartment. Take your things. Begin to prepare it for us. We are no longer welcome in Bassett Place."

"We shouldn't have come in the beginning," Bevis retorted, nodding her pink head. "I told Runyon that, and look what happened."

When Bevis had gone, Theodora repeated her earlier words. "It's crazy."

But Winifred and Alexander were staring at Mickey.

She knew they were waiting for her to say she'd changed her mind, hadn't really meant that they must leave. She knew they hoped she would soften into insincere apologies.

She said nothing.

With a single reproachful glance, Winifred left the room, trailed by Theodora.

Alexander stopped only to say, "I think you're making a mistake."

Mickey poured herself a cup of cold tea.

Her anger was gone now, and with it her confidence that she could do what she knew she must. But her resolution was unaltered.

She left her tea, and went upstairs, touching the note still in her pocket. Whoever had written those black bat track words for her to read must be wondering why she hadn't mentioned them.

She paused to listen to the raised voices she could hear from Winifred's room.

"But why?" Noah was asking.

"You see," Winifred said, "She's not reasonable. Something is wrong with her. Notes, flowers, those clothes, that business with the twins . . . but really, Alexander. Can't you do something?"

"It's not fair," Theodora wailed.

"I don't know," Alexander was obviously answering Winifred's questions. "I just don't know."

Mickey hurried on, ran the narrow stairway to her room.

Now they all knew.

The trap was set.

She had offered herself as bait.

Which one of them would turn a murderer's face to hers? And when? And how?

It was just a little later that she saw Bevis gathering her potted plants from the tiny balcony of the apartment over the garage. Soon after, Bevis loaded the car, and drove away.

Mickey knew that the pink-haired, plump woman was glad to leave Bassett Place, where the memory of Runyon's death remained a burden hard to accept.

As Bevis passed through the gates, there was a tap at Mickey's door.

She turned from the window. "Yes?"

Noah came in. "Mickey, I want to talk to you."

She nodded.

He closed the door behind him. Slouching, hands jammed in his pockets, he asked, "Now what is this all about, Mickey?"

Bottomless dark eyes staring into her.

She tore her gaze away lest she drown in them.

She tore her gaze away, reminding herself that the sweetness she saw might be no more than pretense.

He had been in the house the first time she found the note. He had gone, and the phone calls began. He had worked in Alexander's office and could have known Marty. His very kiss, yes, even the sweetness of his mouth on hers, might have been designed to lull her suspicions, to deceive her.

She answered finally. "I don't know what there is to say. I've asked that your family move out."

"And that applies to me as well?" he demanded stiffly.

She seized upon the obvious, "Well, Noah, I could hardly have you here . . . with your mother gone . . . and besides . . ."

"I don't give a damn for the proprieties." He stared at her, his lithe body rigid. "You suspect me along with the rest of them, don't you, Mickey?"

Her cheeks burned. She didn't try to answer him.

He gave her a mocking smile. "You don't dissemble very well."

She still didn't answer him.

"I wish that you had trusted me," he said in a harsh voice, and left her alone.

She had not thought that she could sleep. But some time during the long, frightening hours of the night, she had fallen into sound and dreamless slumber, and wakened from it, ears straining to listen.

There was nothing, nothing.

But she slowly climbed from her bed, went to get a cigarette. She rolled it unlit between her fingers, thinking of Bennett.

She paused to look out of the window. The lawn, the driveway, the iron fence, was hidden in deepest shadow. Neither moon, nor stars, brightened the shawl of empty dark.

She peered into the night, staring. Suddenly her eyes widened.

The two small gas flames over the big gates were gone.

The lamps of Bassett Place had flickered away.

18

She hesitated in brief indecision.

Did she dare go through the threatening house down into the threatening dark?

Safety was in her room, behind the locked door.

But Runyon had said the flickering gaslights meant that all was well at the Bassett Place, and now the lights were gone.

There was no safety, there could be none, until she knew the truth.

Bennett and Runyon and Marty had died.

Mickey knew that she must be the next victim.

She had offered herself as bait, hoping to lure unknown hands into action. And now, somewhere beyond the locked door of her room, those hands were ready.

She had slept in her clothes.

It took her only a moment to unlock the door.

Another moment to reach the stairs.

She went down them on tiptoe, and around her, the old house seemed to whisper, the shadows seemed to beckon.

The hands were ready, waiting.

She went to meet them.

There was no other way.

Down through the whispering house.

Safely through the hall, and out onto the porch.

There, she paused, breath held.

She heard a faint creak at the stairs. It could have been a movement, a muted footfall. It could have been no more than warping wood.

But she went down into the driveway. She looked toward the big gates. Yes. The flickering gaslights were gone.

She turned to study the house. It rose above her, big, dark, suddenly menacing again.

Then, past the south side, beyond where Runyon had fallen and died, she saw a tiny wink of light. It glowed and faded and glowed again.

A tiny wink of light in the apartment above the garage.

She went toward it as if hypnotized, moving silently through the night mist.

She passed around the aluminum ladder that leaned against the narrow balcony where Bevis had always kept her potted plants.

She paused there, listening again.

Was it the wind, the mist, in the leafless limbs of the shrubbery? Or had someone moved against them?

She turned, gray eyes wide, searching the shadows.

Nothing, nothing.

She went on to the stairs that led through the garage up to the apartment.

From there she could no longer see the window, the winking light. But reflected around her, seeming to come and go with the regularity of a signal beacon, was a faint colorless glimmer.

She climbed the steps, moved silently upward into the shadows of a small porch. The door there was closed, but when she touched it with her fingertips, it swung inward.

She eased her way past it, breath held, eyes searching the flickering shadows.

A tall electric taper stood on the window sill. Its bulb winked on, sent ripples of faint light against the dark. Its bulb winked off, left solid nothingness behind.

She stared at it fascinated.

She stared at it, frozen in terror.

She had offered herself as bait, and the trap had sprung. But she was within the trap. And in that moment, she realized that someone had exploited her weakness, as he had exploited the weaknesses of the others, to destroy her, as he had destroyed them. She had trusted no one. No one at all. Not even herself.

Her fear of the valley of long and living shadows had kept her from seeking help, from telling anyone what was happening around her.

She turned, and with a scream beginning on her lips, she ran for the door.

She saw it moving, drawing back from her reaching fingers. She managed just to touch a splintery edge, and suddenly it slammed in, struck her with the full force of desperate strength behind it. She went spinning away. She tumbled into an obstruction, a piece of furniture, and fell heavily.

There was a whisper of sound in the grotesque blinking dark. She rolled away, and got to her knees. But the huge shifting shadows around her were suddenly gone. The tall electric taper on the window sill, until then signalling in a rise and fall of pale light, went out.

Blinded, afraid to move, she waited, listening.

Beyond her own fear-driven pulses, she heard the night wind stir the bare limbs of the old oaks outside, and then, close by, there was a rustle of cloth, a breath.

By that time, only seconds that had seemed hours, her vision had begun to return. The room developed shape again. And, seeing the hunched shadow near the wall, she knew that she, too, could be seen.

She gasped, threw herself sideways.

But the hunched shadow came at her, huge, enveloping. It dropped over her, a shadow no longer.

It developed weight, substance, and terrible bruising hands.

With no surprise at all, she whispered, "Alexander, it's you. It's always been you."

"You could have made it easy for yourself," he said.

"By marrying you!"

He didn't answer her at once. He was over her, pulling her to her feet. Her arms were wrenched behind her. Her sprained wrist, still sensitive within its tape casing, blazed with sudden pain.

Her brief struggle was useless.

Her hands were tied at her back.

She was thrust onto the sofa, legs wedged under the heavy pillows.

"Just be still," he said. "I've got some things to do."

Pompous efficiency in his voice.

Strangely, even then, she wanted to laugh.

"And if you want to scream . . . go on," he told her. "Nobody can hear you."

"Why, Alexander," she said wonderingly, "You've always hated me, haven't you?"

"If it hadn't been for you, Bassett Place

would have been mine, Mickey."

He had said he had things to do.

She must keep him talking, keep him from doing those things whatever they were.

The outlines of the pattern were quite clear to her now. Yet, keeping her voice soft, steady, she asked, "How did it start, Alexander? Why?"

"I told you why. When you were adopted, what was mine was taken from me. By you, Mickey. I didn't know that, of course, until . . ."

"Until I had the breakdown?"

"I was away at school. But I heard about it. I heard what caused it, too. Mother and Theodora left Bassett Place. They belonged there — we did, not you, Mickey." He took a step away from her.

She said quickly, "But, Alexander, when did it really start."

He laughed. "You know when. The day your parents died. After that . . ." He shrugged. "It was all there, in my mind. The whole thing. Simply waiting to be done. You had had the breakdown. I knew all about that. And Mother had always been fascinated by twins. When I found Dr. Markham's note in your father's papers, I knew why. That was all I needed."

"You came with Noah and Theodora to Copenhagen, and . . . ."

Alexander's blue eyes narrowed. "And
. . . ?"

"I've had the pills analyzed, Alexander. I
know how Bennett died. I even know why
now. It was necessary, wasn't it? Bennett had
to die, because he was my natural heir. He
had to die, and I had to come back to Bassett
Place."

"Of course. I brought the pills with me, not
knowing how easy it would be. But when I
saw the bottle in the desk with his medicine
. . ." Alexander shrugged. "It worked nicely,
too. We three were in the States by the time
it actually happened."

"And just as you intended, I came home."
She went on, "And you had already broken
your engagement to Vivian, I suppose."

Alexander gave Mickey a tight smile. "Not
exactly. Let's say that I delayed things, while
I proceeded with the plan I had already laid
out."

Pompous again. And again, too, she wanted
to laugh.

"But you never intended your proposals to
me seriously, Alexander. You had already
started to try to . . . ."

"You see that, do you?"

It was as if he couldn't resist the chance
to explain, describe, to show how clever he

had been. He had always been that way, she realized.

He went on, "The proposals, the pursuit, all that . . . please don't consider it unflattering, but it was all simply to gain your trust. But, of course, you never trusted anyone. Except Runyon. And Runyon . . ." Alexander shrugged his thick-set shoulders. "That couldn't be helped."

Runyon. Yes, that was right. She had trusted Runyon. She had told him what was happening. And Runyon had died.

She swallowed hard. "The notes, Alexander?"

"It was so simple," he repeated. "Everyone knew you had always been unstable. It was obvious that you would either collapse, or appear to, if handled properly. Which would make it possible for me to take over."

"Incompetent," she whispered.

"The first night, when Winifred and I had come home, I drove back to Bassett Place, left the note. That was the beginning." He shook his head. "It was just as I'd planned. The notes, the flowers, all those phone calls. But you had to tell Runyon. He came to me with the notes. He didn't accuse me outright, you understand. He pretended to be asking my advice. But I knew what he meant. I played along. I said I was sure I could stop it. That evening, when I saw him on the ladder, I took a chance, improvised. I jerked the ladder from under him. And that was that."

"And with Runyon gone, I had no one to turn to," she whispered.

"It was so easy. Marty had worked in my office for a couple of weeks last year. I noticed her resemblance to you then. It helped form my plan. For a sizable sum, she made the phone calls. I never intended that you should meet her, of course."

"Then why did her resemblance to me matter?"

"Because I knew it would frighten you if the shopkeepers, and others, mentioned her resemblance to you. And I knew once you found the letter from Dr. Markham, as I intended you should, that you would start looking for her. I never thought she would dare double-cross me. She talked to you. She met you. She allowed you to talk her into moving into Bassett Place. She decided she could impersonate your dead twin, and that I couldn't do a thing about it." He added grimly, "But I did, and that was easy, too."

"But how did you know what she was going to do?"

"She told me. She warned me not to let on that she was an impostor. Which was her mistake. I picked up a stolen car, collected her, and drove her out to the Palisades. She wasn't suspicious. She thought she had me safely stymied. But from then on . . ." His voice trailed away.

"Yes," Mickey prompted him. "Yes, it just didn't work out, did it?'

But those were the wrong words, she knew at once.

For he backed away from her, disappeared into the shadows. "It is working out," he told her, his voice muffled.

Desperately, she cried, "As soon as I found out about Marty. I realized what was going on. I knew . . ."

"Not quite. You weren't sure who was behind it. And that didn't matter. Because you are quite mad. Everyone knows you're mad. And the mad do strange things."

She heard his movements, the rustle of paper, grunts of effort.

She struggled, but she couldn't move. She couldn't quite see what he was doing in the shadows across the room.

"And that is where you went wrong," she told him, unable, even then, to stifle her triumph.

He had done his worst, but he hadn't driven her back into the valley of long and living shadows.

"True," he said. "I knew I needed much

more time. And the night you said we were trying to drive you mad, I realized I didn't have any time left. So . . ."

"The stairs," she said.

"The stairs. And tonight you told us we had to go. I presume that was because of Bennett's pills."

"Why did you turn out the gaslights?" she asked quickly. For she heard no more movements, no more rustles of paper, and was sure he had nearly finished his preparations.

He came towards her. "To get you out here. You couldn't see this window from your room. But once on the path, checking the lamps, you'd notice my taper. It was just what would appeal to you. And I was right, wasn't I?"

She agreed hopelessly.

But she had been wriggling her wedged legs, and managed to slip her feet from her shoes, which gave her sudden freedom beneath the wedged pillows.

"I would like to make it easy for you," he was saying, "Fire is so unpleasant. But it has to look good, Mickey."

He reached for her, heaved her shoulders up, his fingers busy at her bound wrists.

They were numb, but free.

She sank back, as if still imprisoned by the pillows. She closed her eyes. If he would only leave her . . . just leave her . . .

He said, muttering to himself, "She's here. Her father's papers scattered all over, the kerosene can that Bevis left . . ."

She, listening to his murmur, heard something else. She held herself very still, her breath suspended.

Faintly, from somewhere outside, past his quick mumble, there was a sound.

He flicked his cigarette lighter twice as he walked away from her. The small flame seemed to blaze up, lighting the whole room. The small flame became huge, a red glaring tongue. He was backing to the door, his pudgy face pink.

Acrid smoke, the hiss of fire.

He was a shadow withdrawing.

Mickey told herself to wait.

But instinct flung her up and away from the sofa, kicking the wedging pillows aside.

He rushed toward her, and at the same time the room seemed to explode. The door slammed in. The window shattered. The real shadows became smoky and multiplied.

As he seized her, thrusting her back toward the sofa, he was himself seized. He disappeared for a moment into the smoke. And when he reappeared, she was safe in Noah's arms.

She was miraculously safe within the sweetness of Noah's arms.

Face grim in the light of flame, dark hair tousled, he carried her toward the door.

And Alexander, a shadow in the acrid smoke, came screaming, "Bassett Place is mine!"

He came, screaming, and she could hear her own scream, finally freed.

It was all in terrible slow motion. His voice, his face, his reaching hands.

Noah staggered to keep his feet, to hold her.

And Alexander was suddenly wrenched away, thrown across the room.

At the same time, Noah yelled, "Get out. All of you get out! The place is going up," and carried her through the door.

She heard Ben's, "Yep, we're coming," and wondered briefly, but only briefly, for turning her face into Noah's broad shoulder, she fainted . . .

Where she opened her eyes, there were gentle lips on her cheek, very close bottomless brown eyes watched her. Noah.

But past his shoulder, on the apartment steps, she saw two struggling figures, and cried out as they broke apart. One came tumbling down the steps. The other darted through the flaming doorway, screaming, "It's mine."

Later, she realized that the terrible slow motion in the apartment had taken only seconds. She knew that what seemed the hours of

Alexander's preparation to burn her alive had only been moments, too. That Ben, worried about her, driving past the house, saw dark where gaslight should have flickered. He came into the grounds on foot. The blinking taper troubled him. He'd watched a while, finally climbed the ladder to the balcony, just as the taper went out. He'd listened, waited, trying to think how to free Mickey safely, until, suddenly the cigarette lighter glowed and the room exploded. "Almost waited too long before I went in through that window," he said, whistling softly.

And Noah, holding her, had said, "I always loved you, Mickey. But I knew you had to settle your fears when you came back. Then Alexander moved in. When you seemed to choose him over me, I got sore, I guess. But I realized something was wrong. I started watching. I couldn't figure it out. When you said you were pushed down the steps, I decided to move in. I've been trying since then to keep up with you, checking your room, and so on. Then I found your door open, your bed unoccupied." He'd searched the house, gone outside. The gaslights were out. But by then, too, the taper was out. He went to the apartment simply because there was no place left to look for Mickey. He had climbed the steps, heard Alexander's voice. Almost instantly the window shattered under Ben's kick, and Noah hearing that, threw himself into the room in time to snatch her from Alexander's arms.

But that was much later, after the fire trucks had washed the flames away, and Alexander's charred body had been found among the ashes of Benjamin Bassett's papers.

It was after Winifred had stared at Mickey, cried, "But it was in your blood . . . If only you'd married Alexander, if only you'd promised to . . . then we could have stayed here together," and then, collapsing into Theodora's arms, "It's all my fault. I didn't know what he was doing, I didn't, but my greed and pride turned him into a murderer!"

When dawn came, and the night mists melted away, Mickey looked out of her window, remembering that Bennett had once told her, "There is no antidote to fear but courage, no anodyne to pain but time," and she knew that he had been trying to urge her out of the cocoon of her childhood. And later he had said the way to resolve doubt was to search for certainty, and she knew that he had had no doubt at all. He hadn't been afraid to tell her that some day she must go home.

Below her, over the iron gates, two pinpoints of flame began to dance within their old-fashioned lamps.

She leaned forward, gray eyes widening.

All was well in Bassett Place again.

Then Noah emerged from the oak trees. He looked up at her, raised his hand.

She swung away from the window, and ran to meet him.